jill marshall

recently moved from the United Kingdom to New Zealand, along with her small daughter and her even smaller mad dog. Her childhood ambition was to become an author, so in 2001 Jill gave up her career as training director at a huge international company to concentrate on writing for children. When not working, writing and being a mum, Jill plays guitar, takes singing lessons and is learning to play the drum kit she has set up in the garage. One day she might even sing in a band again . . .

Look out for the sequel:

jane blonde spies trouble

Jane Blonde
sensational spylet

JILL MARSHALL

MACMILLAN CHILDREN'S BOOKS

First published 2006 by Macmillan Children's Books
a division of Macmillan Publishers Limited
20 New Wharf Road, London N1 9RR
Basingstoke and Oxford
www.panmacmillan.com

Associated companies throughout the world

ISBN-13: 978-0-330-43814-8
ISBN-10: 0-330-43814-X

5 7 9 8 6

A CIP catalogue record for this book is available from
the British Library.

Typeset by Nigel Hazle
Printed and bound in Great Britain by Mackays of Chatham plc, Kent

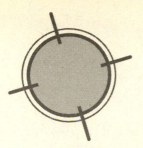

love, thanks and g-mamma raps to glenys bean and rachel denwood for their support, enthusiasm and scary amounts of expertise; to kelly mckain, jayne sambrook smith, kathy white and my mum and dad for talking me down off the ceiling whenever necessary; and to family and friends on both sides of the globe for having faith and lending me money.

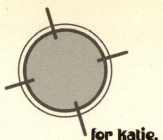

for katie, my own blonde-girl,
with all love, always

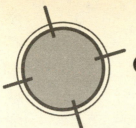

contents

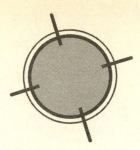

'It really is a mouse,' said the man to the kitten.

The little cat sniffed suspiciously. Afraid, the mouse sprang away like a jack-in-the-box, as the cat arched his tawny back and hissed.

The man laughed, then let out a long sigh. 'I think it's time now, little kitty. We have to go away. I've started something that, well, someone else has to finish.'

As he gathered up the mouse and popped it back into its cage, the cat watched him warily.

'You've every right to look nervous, my friend. Part of me hoped this moment would never arrive. But it's here. And I have no choice. Let's go . . .'

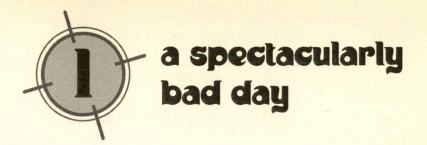

a spectacularly bad day

'Oh no! How could my trainers have melted?'

Just hours earlier, when Janey Brown had hung up her PE bag in the cloakroom, there had been a pair of sturdy little black running shoes nestled in the cotton sack like a couple of plump baby blackbirds. Now her bag contained two flat discs of rubber with tatty bits of cloth flapping around on the top. Her trainers had actually melted.

'Why me?' Janey moaned. 'Why is it always me these days?'

She pressed a finger on to her tear duct to stop herself crying, but a small droplet still managed to squeeze out on to her nose. It always did. Anyway, today Janey felt she had the right to cry, just a bit. Her spectacularly bad day had started almost as soon as she left home that morning, when the postman tried to stop her taking her own letter.

'But it's addressed to me!' Janey had pointed at the scribbled name on the large white envelope.

'Well, I suppose,' the postman replied unhelpfully. She couldn't see much of his face; his peaked cap was pulled down tight against his nose. For a moment, though, his mouth opened and closed in confusion. In fact, thought Janey, he looked a bit like a nervous goldfish. Dark rings of sweat edged from his grey armpits towards his maroon collar.

Must be his first day, she thought. Janey knew all about first days. She had started at a new school only a couple of weeks ago and it had been pretty scary.

Suddenly the postman grinned and pointed at the postmark. 'Not paid enough for it, have they, whoever sent it? Look, it's only got two stamps and it should have, errrr, four. I'd better take it back to the office.'

Janey looked at the envelope. It did have only two stamps, but someone had scrawled between them the number four and then two quarter signs. Janey, however, barely glanced at that as she recognized the smiley face of her uncle Solomon beaming at her from the postmark. Her uncle owned the ice-lolly manufacturer Sol's Lols, and a drawing of his round face was the company's logo. Even though Janey had never actually met him, her uncle Solomon did sometimes send her presents. And here was a letter from him!

'Look,' she said, trying to tug the envelope out of the postman's grip, 'those numbers must mean I owe you another four and a half pence. I haven't got a five-pence piece, but I can give you ten.'

'Haven't got any change,' smirked the postman, pulling harder.

'You can keep the extra money!'

Janey gave the letter one last pull and at last it slipped from the postman's grasp. She'd been pulling with such force that her fist flew backwards and she smacked herself in the face. Her eyes smarted painfully and tears spurted down her nose. The postman looked doubtfully, first at Janey and then at the letter, then abruptly scurried off, pulling out his mobile phone.

'Hey!' called Janey. 'Please don't report me to the post office. I wanted to pay you the extra money, honestly!'

It was too late. He had already disappeared round the corner.

Janey stuffed the letter into her bag. There was no time to read it now – she was already in danger of missing the school bell. Which would mean more bad luck. Janey just couldn't believe how much of it she'd had since moving house and starting at the new school. She'd never been unpopular at her last school. In fact she'd had quite a few friends – even though she was pretty shy – but here no one wanted to get to know her. Everyone seemed confident and clever and happy with the people they had already paired up with. Maybe if she hadn't started one term into the year she'd have had a better chance. But no. None of the other kids was interested in Janey, and she was beginning to feel she might as well have 'Boringly normal and normally boring' stamped across her forehead.

And someone obviously agreed with her. They'd even said so, though not to her face. After only a few days at Winton School, little notes in distinctive rounded handwriting had started to appear in her bag, or on her chair, or even pinned to the back of her jumper.

> POOR OLD JANEY - BROWN BY NAME
> AND BROWN BY NATURE.

> IF JANEY BROWN WAS ANY MORE BORING
> SHE'D BE INVISIBLE.

> JANEY BROWN WILL NOT BE IN SCHOOL TODAY.
> THE UGLY-POLICE HAVE HER LOCKED UP FOR
> THE SAKE OF THE REST OF US.

Janey had no idea who was writing the notes, or why. She only knew that they were making her hate the idea of getting up in the morning. And they didn't exactly help her cause with the other kids. The notes were so embarrassing, like Janey's very worst nightmare, the one she had when she was feeling really anxious. It was pretty much a nightly event at the moment – *she opens her eyes, it's dark, and then suddenly a spotlight falls on her and she's standing on the school stage, alone, singing the national anthem, but she's in fancy dress, and not just any old fancy dress but the fairy outfit she wore when she was five years old, and as her eyes adjust she can see that everyone is sniggering at the straining seams of the pink tutu, at her voice which sounds like a cat in yowling, terrible pain . . .*

Janey reached the school, bile rising in her throat. It was tempting to continue past the wrought-iron gates and not go in at all. With a sigh, she hoisted her bag on to her shoulder and stepped across the threshold into the school grounds, just as a small body cannoned straight into her, sending her flailing on to the floor.

'Watch out, idiot!' The small boy in slightly too-short grey trousers glared at her indignantly.

'It wasn't . . . I didn't . . . sorry!'

'You should watch where you're going, dreamy,' said the boy gruffly, shoving one of Janey's books back into her bag for her.

Janey felt terrible, even though she was fairly sure that it hadn't been her fault. 'I know. I was in a bit of a dream. Well, more of a nightmare really. Hope I didn't hurt you. Look, you don't need to do that.' She grabbed her belongings together hurriedly. 'Better go. Don't want to be late as well as . . . everything else.'

'Yeah, whatever.'

Hands in pockets, the boy turned away from the school gates and wandered down the street, trying to look very grown up with his shoulders back and his feet stepping away in a steady saunter. Janey couldn't help smiling at the little boy, trying to act like a big man and not quite getting it right. Feeling slightly more cheery, she took a deep breath and walked into school.

There were no nasty notes that day but still Janey didn't have a single conversation with anyone. No chats about what she'd done last night (mostly some puzzles in one of her beloved books of dingbats). No worrying together about homework. No offers to swap her disgusting ketchup sandwiches for something less, well, disgusting. But at least it was peaceful.

Until that last lesson of the day, when Janey reached into her PE bag and discovered that the Someone-Who-Had-It-In-For-Her had got there first.

She pulled the liquefied trainers out of her bag and peered underneath. Nothing had escaped her enemy's attention. Janey's navy shorts looked like they had been put through a shredding machine and now lined the bag like hamster-bedding. Her regulation white aertex top had been wodged into a sticky ball with what appeared to be treacle.

Her whole PE bag was a disaster area.

A bit like Janey Brown's entire life.

2 not-so-fairy godmother

'Brown! Are you in here?'

Janey winced. It was Alfie Halliday, Class Superstar. Most of the other kids made Janey nervous, but Alfie was so horribly *capable* that he made her feel even more of a klutz than ever.

He strode into the changing rooms towards her.

'So you are here. Why didn't you answer me? Miss Rale wants you out on the field right now, or you are in real trouble. Even more than usual,' he added.

'But I can't!' Janey gulped. 'Someone's melted my PE kit!'

Alfie's eyebrows shot up as he stared at Janey. 'What? Try giving that excuse to the teacher – I'm sure it'll go down brilliantly. Not.'

It's all right for you, Mr Popular! thought Janey poisonously as she slunk after him. Alfie was clever and sporty, with brown eyes and thick hair that gleamed like a conker, quite the opposite of Janey's thin, rat-coloured locks. On top of all that, he was the headmistress's son and therefore Untouchable.

Janey shuffled towards Miss Rale. Her new teacher looked at her kindly.

'What's up, Janey?' she asked, wrinkling her nose. Janey thought how young and kind her teacher looked in her PE skirt, with a whistle on a string around her neck. She was new to the school too, and seemed to be the only person with any interest in Janey.

'Someone's melt . . . er, I can't find . . . I mean, I've brought the wrong bag with me and I haven't got my PE kit. I'm really sorry.'

Miss Rale sighed gently. 'OK, Janey, don't worry. Look, it's nearly home time. If you sit on the bench near the gates I can keep an eye on you, and you can be first out at the end of the day.'

'Oh! Thanks, miss.'

With a sigh Janey fetched her PE bag from the cloakroom. She almost cried again as she folded herself on to the hard bench at the gate. She felt ashamed: ashamed that she couldn't do anything about the horrid notes; ashamed that she was so boring and unattractive that she hadn't made a single friend in over a fortnight; and ashamed most of all because right at that moment, more than anything else in the world, she really, really wanted her mum.

'Pity your mother's not here right now, isn't it?'

Someone had taken the words right out of Janey's head. Swivelling round, her eyes fell upon a woman standing on the other side of the railings. With a grin as wide as Janey's whole head, she looked like a cross between a hugely friendly auntie and a completely scary maniac.

'Wh-what did you say?' asked Janey, taking in the enormous wobbling body squeezed into a stretchy pink miniskirt, clinging leopard-print top, tied-up headscarf and long black wellies. Mottled flesh frothed around the woman's knees like a milkshake, and a heavily made-up face beamed out from beneath an explosion of bubbly fair hair.

The woman waggled her ringed fingers at Janey, booming away in her loud, twangy voice. 'I was just thinking, what a shame it is that your mother's not here right now. She'd know how to deal with all of this, wouldn't she?'

Janey thought about it. It was true: her mum was very ordinary, but she did always know how to make Janey feel better.

'Erm, yes, I suppose so. Mum would be able to help.'

'Thought so!' replied the woman brightly, pulling a fluffy brown scarf from her bag and swirling it around her neck. The scarf had dangly strips hanging off it at intervals and a little face attached to the end of it like an old-fashioned fox fur. It looked uncomfortably lifelike, as if at any moment one eye would open and stare malevolently at passers-by, and especially at Janey. 'I knew it. Always top of the class, your mother, Janey. Quite the star.'

'You . . . you know her? And me?'

The woman stared at Janey very hard for a moment, a curious expression on her face.

'Indeed I do, Janey. Hot diggety dog, I do! I know you're zany Janey because I'm . . . well, I'm your godmother.'

Mouth wide open, Janey mentally rattled through the sorry straggle of relatives that had turned up over the years. There was Uncle James, who worked 'in the City'. Janey had met him only a few times. And then there was Uncle Solomon, the brother of her dead father, who sent fabulous gifts and letters on odd occasions but whom Janey had never ever seen. Nobody had mentioned a godmother of any kind, particularly one who looked like a crazy bag lady.

'Never heard of me, have you, babes? Not heard of your lovely groovy godmother?'

Dubiously, Janey shook her head. The woman shrugged her bag up on to her shoulder and peered seriously left and right along the street.

'OK. But you've heard of Solomon's Polifical Investigations.'

'Er, no. No, I haven't. I've got an uncle called Solomon, but he makes ice lollies. Not . . . polly-wolly wotsits.'

The woman shook her head with irritation, jowls wobbling like a bloodhound's.

'Well, I've got to say, girly-girl, that it's a shifty old shame you understand so little. Because it's going to make the next bit a who-o-o-le lot more difficult to explain. You see, I was just coming to find out what Solomon had to say to you when he got in touch. But there's been a bit of a hiccup. I've now been directed to let you know that right now your dear mother's in a bit of a pickle. In fact, it's bigger than a pickle. More like a great green gherkin. Yes indeedy. So you're going to have to rescue her. You have to come with me, zippety split. R-r-r-r-right now.'

Janey almost fell to the ground, so eager was she to get off the bench and run back to Miss Rale. This woman was clearly nuts. 'I can't! I'm not allowed! We've had lessons about stranger danger and . . . and all that!'

'Sweety, I am not a stranger! I've told you! I've been sent by your dear uncle's organization, Solomon's Polificational Investigations. Call it SPI, saves time. And I'm your godmother! Although, being the young groovster that I am, I've come up with something a little less boring. Call me . . . G-Mamma.'

'*G-Mamma?*'

'Yeah, G-Mamma. You know, like, jiving, hip-hopping street-talk.'

'Er. Sorry. I don't know what you're on about.'

'Rapping! You know, like:

'My name's G-Mamma, and I've come to say,
You'd better get your booty underway.
Your ma's in trouble, it's plain to see.
And who's gonna help her? Janey B!'

Janey sat with her jaw hanging open. G-Mamma sighed. 'Well, I can see there are all sorts of areas in which you need educating. You're not very hip and happening, young Janey, are you? What have they

13

been teaching you? Oh, forget it – time for all that later. Right now, you need to rescue Gina.'

Janey shook her head again. 'Gina? Who's that?'

'Gina Bellarina, darling. Your mother?'

A huge feeling of relief swept over Janey. This mad woman had obviously got the wrong person.

'My mother's name is *Jean*. Jean Brown. You must have made a mistake.'

G-Mamma's heavily glossed lips curled in distaste. 'Jean Brown? Good gawdy Lordy, has she gone back to that boring old identity? Oh, Janey. There's even more to do than I thought. And you're just wasting time. You can't dilly around on all your missions like this, you know.'

Janey was positive now that the woman was completely stark-staring loopy. She probably stopped people in cinema queues and at bus stops all the time, dribbling on about missions and dangerous situations. And on this spectacularly bad day, wasn't it just typical that Mad Blubber Woman happened to have chosen Janey's school to drop in on?

Gathering up her PE bag, Janey stepped away from the bench. 'Look, I don't want to be rude or anything, but I can't come with you. My mum's going to be here to collect me any minute now, and I'll have to—'

'No, she won't,' interrupted G-Mamma, inspecting her purple fingernails and starting to look a little bored. 'Haven't you been listening? You'll have to take more notice of your G-Mamma in future, you know, child. Your poor mother is currently on the roof of your Uncle

James's bank in the City. Furthermore, she is about to be toppled off it by a couple of Sinerlesse Group members. And I don't need to tell you – well, maybe I do – that the Sinerlesse Group are pure eeeeeeeeevil. Your mum is in trouble as big as it gets, unless you get your bony behind down to that bank sharpish and rescue her like the Spylet you are!'

Janey's head whirled. Her mum certainly hadn't shown up at the school gates yet, and she was never, ever late. But what was this G-Mamma ranting about? SPI? The Sinerlesse Group? Spylets? Janey looked round jerkily, but could only see Alfie Halliday swaggering by with his mates.

There was not a single friend to help Janey decide what to do. But instead of wanting to cry, she felt as if a mist had suddenly cleared in her head.

She had three options. She could do nothing – but what if her mother really was in danger? She could go with G-Mamma, hoping that she was not an escaped lunatic but a genuine friend of Uncle Solomon's, like she'd said. The woman did seem to know a lot about Janey's family. Or Janey could come up with her own brilliant plan. And like a small, bright explosion in her brain, that very plan occurred to her.

'All right. Here's what I'll do. I can't come with you, but if Mum isn't here soon or at home, I'll meet you at Uncle James's bank at 4.30 p.m. With the police.'

G-Mamma snorted. 'Police? What can they do that you can't? Don't bother with those by-the-book bores. And I think you'd better make it four o'clock, girl! Gina's in more danger with every second that passes.'

This is so mad, thought Janey, closing her eyes as she started to feel slightly faint.

When she opened them again, G-Mamma was gone.

bikes and bashed knees

After ten minutes, Janey was still alone at the school gates. Chewing her lip nervously, she glanced at her watch. It was already half past three. Her mother was at least fifteen minutes late. With one last desperate look along the street in search of their little yellow car, Janey started to walk, then jog, then canter home with her lank hair and disastrous PE bag streaming out behind her.

Their rickety wooden gate banged against the wall as she pelted through. It was tiny, like the house. Janey and her mum had needed to move to a smaller house when the money from her father's will began to run out. They'd tried to make the most of things, holding the hugest of garage sales and going to the cinema with some of the proceeds. Now Janey's mum had taken on two jobs just to make sure they could still have some little luxuries, like fish and chips on a Friday night. Luckily, a cleaning job had practically fallen into her mum's lap, out of the blue, paying her more than any other job she'd ever had. She'd been so cheerful about it all, but Janey knew her mum was worried behind her smile.

She couldn't bear the thought that her lovely mum might be in trouble. Yelling like a warrior about to go into battle, Janey charged up the path.

'Mum! Mum! Where are you? Open the door!'

There was no reply. Wishing she was allowed to have her own key, Janey pounded on the door.

'Do you mind? You're lowering the tone of the neighbourhood, you young hooligan!' Mr Harris, their elderly next-door neighbour, was leaning out of his upstairs window. 'I've got someone coming to look at buying the house soon – I don't want them thinking they'd have to live with this racket!'

'Sorry, Mr H!' shouted Janey. 'But I can't get in. And I can't find my mum. Have you seen her?'

The old man nodded smugly. 'Yes, and she looked pretty upset at whatever those two men were saying to her, I can tell you. Ran straight to her car and took off like a lunatic, she did. Had to come and close the front door for her myself!'

Janey swallowed hard. 'What two men, Mr H?'

'Well, these two chaps. Very smart, in suits. Looked like bank managers.'

'Oh, no!' All Janey's breath left her chest in a mighty rush.

So maybe it was true. Perhaps something *had* happened to her mother. What if that G-Mamma woman was right? Would she, Janey Brown, have to go to her mum's rescue? Mr Harris's voice drifted back to her.

'. . . mind clearing up? Move that dreadful old bike

18

out of the front? I am trying to create a good impression for buyers!'

Jayne looked around quickly. Her mother's old bike, thick with rust and cobwebs, was sprawled against the hedge. Janey thought they'd sold it in the garage sale, but obviously not. Pulling it from the hedge, Janey brushed away the spiders with a shudder. She hated riding bikes. She particularly hated this one as the handlebars were too low for her long legs and knocked against her knees. But with only twelve minutes to go until the four o'clock meeting at Uncle James's bank, Janey knew the only way to get across town through the traffic was to get on and pedal as if her life – or someone else's – depended on it.

Stuffing her PE bag into the large basket hanging from the handlebars, Janey wheeled the bike out through the gate, climbed on and pushed off from the kerb. It was not just the bike-riding that concerned her; she had only ever been to Uncle James's bank a couple of times before, and each time she had travelled on the underground with her mum.

'Which way? Which way?' she moaned to herself as she jolted along the gutter.

Terrified, Janey forced herself out into the traffic. Cars and motorbikes zoomed past on each side. She wobbled and shook, painfully skinning her left knee on the bottom of the wicker basket.

'Oh, I don't know! Think, Janey, think!'

Screeching to a shaky stop at the end of the road, she felt like screaming with frustration. Then, to her left, she spotted the sign for the local underground station and her brain seemed to clear.

'Bikes can go on the underground!'

Janey was so anxious to get to her mother as quickly as she could that she didn't even get off her bike to go down into the station. Not normally the kind of girl to do anything naughty, she tucked her head into her collar as she bounced painfully through the station and down the stone steps, praying that no one would recognize her. Luckily it was too early for people to be coming out of work, so the stairs were clear enough for her to rattle down, shouting, 'Excuse me, please! Sorry! Would you mind?' to anyone who got in her way. She whizzed past the open-mouthed guard, screaming, 'Don't worry, I've got a pass!' And suddenly she was on the platform.

Janey paused for a moment to push her mousy, now slightly sweaty, fringe out of her eyes and gazed up at the arrivals board. A couple of people caught her eye and turned away hurriedly, shuffling down the platform as if they couldn't see her.

Great. I must look as crazy as G-Mamma, Janey thought.

The arrivals news was not good either: ten minutes until the next train.

'Oh, I don't have time for this!' she shouted to no one in particular. 'What am I going to do? I have to get to Uncle James's bank!'

As she spoke, Janey was amazed to feel the bike start to shake. Thinking there must be a train coming, she gripped the handlebars and prepared to ride it through the open doors on to the carriage. But to her horror, she found her feet skidding along the shiny platform as the bike slid towards the edge. Crying out, she dug her heels in to stop the bike vaulting on to the rails, but it was unstoppable. Janey's feet dangled in mid-air and with a lurch she tipped forwards on to the track. The bike teetered precariously on its front wheel for a moment, then crashed back down with both tyres planted firmly on the train track.

Two waiting passengers screamed and huddled back against the platform wall. The sound of the screams only reminded Janey of the danger her mother could be in, and all at once her fear left her. Fierce determination took its place as she positioned her feet firmly on the pedals.

'All right, Mum – I'm coming!'

She set off along the track. Once she had got into a rhythm, Janey found that the bumping wasn't too bad, and although it was pitch black in the tunnel she could see the glint of the rails that ran either side of her, reflecting the twin dynamo lights glowing on her handlebars. She knew she had to stay exactly in the middle of the tracks if she didn't want to get herself electrocuted, but by pedalling very fast she could make the bike stay completely upright, with barely a wobble or a bump. After just a minute or so of pedalling, Janey shot through a station, to the astonishment of the passengers on the platform. After three more minutes she passed through another one, travelling at such an amazing speed that she only just managed to look at the sign as it flashed by.

'Wow! Next station already!'

Janey pressed on breathlessly, but beneath the wheels the ground was beginning to judder. A roaring sound filled Janey's ears and she shook with the effort of keeping the bike between the two rails. But as fast as she pedalled, she still could not outpace the train that was bearing down on her. Daring to glance over her shoulder, Janey saw the bright light of the cabin just metres behind her, close enough for her to register the look of terror and astonishment on the driver's face. Janey knew that this was it. She wouldn't be able to save her mum. What had she been thinking? She couldn't even save herself.

The wheels of the bike sped round as the thunderous train inched closer. Janey screamed as the train touched her back mudguard with a shriek like a dentist's drill. Then the nudge of the train catapulted the bike up through the air, spinning it towards a crescent of white light.

'A bright light! That must be heaven!' cried Janey, screwing her eyes tight as she waited for the crunch.

For long seconds it felt as though she was floating in thick, eerie silence. Then with a deafening crash she landed on a huge heap of shopping bags.

Three anxious faces peered at her.

'Is . . . is this heaven?' asked Janey, wondering why she hurt so much if she was dead.

'Heaven?' replied an old lady in a quavering voice. 'No, dear. This is Blackfriars.'

'I made it!'

'Made it? You squashed my tropical fruits! What'll I do with my mangoes now?' squeaked another lady.

Janey extracted her PE bag from the mangled mess of the bike. 'Erm, make chutney? Sorry, got to rush! I've got to save someone.'

And she hobbled up the stairs into the fading daylight.

mad clambers

Uncle James's office was just a minute's walk from the station, but Janey was so shaken and bruised that she had to force herself to take each step. She had speeded up to a sort of hobble-lurch, hobble-lurch across the cobbles when she spotted the large, semicircular courtyard that led to the revolving door of the bank's reception area.

There was no way through. Every bit of space was taken up with people – bank employees who seemed to have been evacuated from the building and who were now shushing each other and pointing towards the front of the crowd. Pushing through, Janey was amazed to discover who was directing the evacuation.

G-Mamma with a megaphone was exceptionally loud, and her audience was completely enthralled by the foghorn woman in her rainbow clothes.

'The fire brigade is on its way,' G-Mamma yelled. 'And even though we're sure it's just a false alarm, the engines are going to need to get right up to the building, which means we have to move all you lovely people somewhere else. As it's four o'clock already, my suggestion as your . . . um, Director of Security . . . would be that you all go home right away. You won't be able to get back in for several hours anyway, until I and my team have done all our checks.'

G-Mamma frowned menacingly at the person who thought *he* was in charge of security, daring him to challenge her. Then she spotted Janey in the crowd.

'Ah, Janey,' she bellowed, 'you made it. Hot stuff, girly-girl! Now we can really get on with everything. Go on, you lot, get lost then. CLEAR OFF IMMEDIATELY, YOU NAMBY-PAMBY NEWTS IN SUITS!'

Perplexed, but pleased to be getting time off work, the bank employees drifted away. Janey walked up to G-Mamma, gently grabbing the end of the megaphone before she could honk through it again.

'Where's my mum? What's all this about?'

G-Mamma pointed upwards. 'She's on the roof, like I said. You'll have to get up there, Spylet.'

'OK.'

Spylet? Hadn't G-Mamma called her that before? But Janey had no time to think about it now – her mum needed her. As she stepped towards the revolving door, she suddenly felt a chubby be-ringed hand on her shoulder.

'Janey, Janey. What is the first rule of combat in your job?'

'G-Mamma,' snapped Janey, using the strange name with hardly a blink, 'I haven't got a job. I'm not even at secondary school yet. What are you on about?'

G-Mamma sighed. 'I can't believe how little you've been taught. Surely your Uncle Sol didn't wipe your mother's memory completely? Unreal! I really am going to have to tell you *everything* myself. The first rule of combat is: "Surprise, surprise, surprise." Don't do the obvious. Catch the enemy unawares. Bamboozle them!'

'So are you saying,' said Janey, staring at G-Mamma, 'that I can't take the lift?'

G-Mamma slapped her hand against her thigh, causing large ripples under her stretchy pink skirt. 'Exactly! That's just what they'll be expecting, isn't it?'

'The stairs, then?'

'Nope. That's what they'll be expecting next.'

Janey was feeling angrier and angrier. Her mother was apparently trapped on the roof of an eight-storey building, with goodness knows who holding her there, and G-Mamma was talking nonsense about her family and setting riddles.

'G-Mamma, can't you just tell me? I need to help my mum. If can't go up in the lift or use the stairs, and I haven't got a helicopter to drop me off up there, would you please tell me how to get on to the roof!'

G-Mamma pursed her lips and suctioned them in and out. Finally she huffed and nodded to herself. 'OK. I was going to make you work it out for yourself, but you're not sufficiently trained yet, and there really isn't time to get you using your normality-befuddled brain properly. The way to get up to the roof is . . . use the SPI-cycle.'

'The spicicle?' It sounded like popsicle. Janey imagined a curry-flavoured ice lolly and pulled a face.

'Not spicicle. SPI-cycle. Like bi-cycle.' G-Mamma sighed.

'Oh, you mean the bike!'

G-Mamma nodded, folding her arms across her enormous bosom. 'Slightly old model, but it will get you up the side of the building without too much trouble. I left it for you, next to the hedge.'

'I know!' Janey groaned. She remembered how smoothly and rapidly the bike had ridden the train tracks, how steadily it had held her between the two electric rails. But could the bike really climb up the side of a building? Janey would never know. 'Look, G-Mamma, it's a fantastic bike. But it's broken. I had to leave it at the station.'

Under the twin circles of blusher on her cheeks, G-Mamma turned pale. 'The bike's broken? How? Solomon preserve us, that's another damaged gadget. I'll be demoted! Goodness, I don't have any other way planned! Your mother is up there at the mercy of two Sinerlesse Group henchmen, and, zany Janey, I'll say it again, they are B. A. D. Baaaaaaaad! You are the only one who can save her. What are you going to do?'

Janey's chest started to heave dangerously. 'I don't know! Can't you climb up to her somehow?'

'Me? Climb? Do I look like an athlete?' snorted G-Mamma, her blue eyes round as pies. 'I mean, I could *be* a trampoline, but there's no way I could *use* one. Anyway, I'm a SPI:KE. I'm not allowed to *carry out* operations, only assist in them. No, girly-girl, if there's any climbing to be done, then sure as lollies are cold, you're the one who has to do it!'

Her grey eyes misting with tears, Janey stared up at the sheer glass sides of the bank building. It was impossible – only a lizard would be able to grip on to those walls. Her only option was to do 'the obvious' and go up in the lift. G-Mamma could like it or lump it.

But just as Janey headed for the revolving door, she heard a shout from high above her. Her mother sounded angry and very, very shrill. What if she put her in even more danger by stepping out of the lift on to the roof? Janey stopped dead in her tracks, and suddenly, for the second time that day, there was a small, searing flash inside her brain.

'All right. I've thought of a way. It's completely insane, but I have to try.'

G-Mamma stared dumbly as Janey reached into her PE bag. Grabbing a melted plimsoll in each hand, she pressed them against the treacly ball of her PE shirt, before slinging the bag back over her shoulder. Then, sliding her fingers under the tattered cloth flaps on the top of each sticky rubber disc, she reached out a hand and touched the glass wall of the building.

It held. Stuck to the pane by one hand, Janey reached her other arm over her head and smacked the second disc on to the glass too. That stuck as well. As she pulled the first hand off and stretched it above the second, she swung her body up the glass so that her feet left the ground and she found herself hanging on to the side of the bank like a long, pale slug.

'Yo! Go, Janey! Go, Janey!' shouted G-Mamma from beneath her, making hideous hip gyrations like a sackful of cheerleaders.

Janey glanced at her, but quickly decided that if she was going to do this, she had better not look down. After a few more suck-and-pulls, she was on a level with the roof of the nearby church, about a quarter of the way up the bank building.

Wondering if it would be more dangerous or less to climb with her eyes closed, Janey forced herself to go on lifting one hand above the other, dragging her weight up behind her. After a few minutes the muscles in her arms were burning, and Janey had to bite her lip hard to stop herself from crying out. She continued to climb until she could no longer hear a single word of whatever G-Mamma was chanting from the ground. By now Janey could see into the roof gardens of the neighbouring buildings. She must be near the top. But she only had the strength to move each disc a few centimetres at a time. She was really straining now, slowing down dramatically . . .

But there it was again – her mother's voice.

'I won't keep repeating myself. My husband is dead. Solomon Brown is his brother. But we are not in contact, and I have absolutely no idea what you're talking about.'

A mean, rough voice hissed just above Janey's head: whoever was holding her mother must be standing close to the edge of the roof. 'And I suppose,' said the voice, 'you have nothing to do with his little enterprises?'

'Nothing at all. Surprising though it may seem, I don't know much about frozen food. But I do believe Sol always was a clever chap, so it doesn't surprise me that he went into business.'

'Do you think we're fools?' barked a second voice. 'We are the Sinerlesse, not simpletons. It's not business, it's espionage! Spying! And you're in on it with Brown. He's already been betrayed by one of his so-called allies. We know he's got a secret worth stealing, so you might as well tell us what you know. Because if you don't you'll be taking a flying jump any minute now, lady.'

Janey gasped, inching closer to the roof. She could tell her mother was really angry by the way she was using her posh telephone voice.

'I am a cleaner and a part-time chiropodist's receptionist! Unless you think anyone's interested in spying on Mrs Phillips having her corns done, I suspect you have confused me with someone else!'

Peeping over the row of bricks edging the roof terrace, Janey stared in amazement. Her mother was tied to an executive leather chair with what looked like a string of fairy lights. Her neat white blouse was torn at the collar, while her sensible skirt was edging up her tan tights. She was trying to sit delicately, knees together, as the two men on either side of her spun the chair backwards and forwards to face each of them in turn.

A tall, thin man with a straggle of fair hair had his back to Janey, his shirt clinging damply to his skin so the cotton had turned almost black. He raised his hands at the shorter man, who was wearing a dark red jacket.

'This is getting us nowhere. Maybe Solomon's de-memorized her or something. Let's chuck her over.'

But the other man was not prepared to give up yet. In a jerky movement he swivelled the leather chair back towards him. 'Look, perhaps I can help jog your memory. If you're bluffing, you'll be very sorry. The Sinerlesse Group does not appreciate time-wasters. And we always get what we want. Now maybe, just maybe, you're not working for Solomon,' he growled, 'but what about the Spylet?'

'Spylet?' Janey's mother asked incredulously. 'Are you completely deranged? What is a Spylet?'

'Oh, come on, you know what a Spylet is! You are making me very impatient, lady! Ariel demands to know. Did. Your. Spylet. Daughter. Decode. Solomon's secret message?'

With every clipped word the man gave the fairy lights a little twist. The sharp glass centres were starting to prick into Mrs Brown's flesh. But Janey's mother was defiant.

'Now just you leave my daughter out of this! Janey has enough to worry about already, growing up without a father and starting new schools and finding no friends. She does not need upsetting any further! Do you hear me?'

The short man's shoulders rounded, straining

his maroon jacket so far that the stitches down the back seam stretched to breaking point. Janey felt sure he was about to attack her mum. It was now or never. With a huge grunt she hoisted herself over the wall, rolling on to the roof behind him.

'Mum! Look out!'

Ignoring her mother's astounded expression, Janey shook off the suction pads and reached into her PE bag. The stocky man spun round and headed towards her. Janey shoved her fist at him, flinging a handful of shredded navy skirt, sticky with treacle, into his face so that he couldn't see a thing. He ran to and fro, hollering and scrabbling wildly at his face.

'My eyes! My eyes! What is this stuff?'

Janey pushed him away, towards an open skylight, and reached for the last remaining item in her bag as the tall, thin man loped across the roof towards her. She quickly made a ball of her sticky PE shirt and threw it at him. It stuck to the rooftop in front of his outstretched leg and, before he could stop his foot landing in it, the man found himself glued to the spot. He was unable to run, except in a half-circle with one foot stuck fast. He dropped to the ground, cursing wildly and trying to free his foot.

'Quick, Mum!' yelled Janey, yanking at the fairy lights. 'Come on!'

Grabbing her mother's hand, Janey pulled her through a door that stood in a little turret in the middle of the roof. They sped down one flight of stairs and found themselves in a corridor. And there, standing like a technicolour usherette with a broad smile on her face, was G-Mamma.

'Come on! It's fine to go *down* in the lift – they won't be expecting *that.*'

Bewildered, Janey's mum allowed herself to be dragged into the lift, stopping only to complain about how dirty and sticky Janey's hands were. They plummeted towards the ground. As they shot through the sliding doors, Janey heard the ping of the bell: the Sinerlesse henchmen on the roof had freed themselves and were now on their way down.

But the men were too slow. As they hurtled out through the revolving door, Janey saw a low, sleek car parked in the courtyard. She glanced quickly at G-Mamma, who simply nodded and pointed a remote control towards it. After she had pushed her mother on to the back seat, Janey threw herself in and slammed the door shut. G-Mamma hurried to the driver's seat, activated the central locking and sped away, just as the men shot out of the building and skittered on to the cobbles.

Once they were a safe distance away, G-Mamma started to shake with laughter. 'Whoo! Check you out, SPI-girl! What a natural you are, Janey! A hot-shot, pot-shot Spylet! Oh, yes! Your first run-in with the Sinerlesse and you made mincemeat of them. Ha!' She wiped tears away from her eyes. 'Reminds you of the old days, doesn't it, Gina?'

Janey's mother shrugged herself into an upright position. 'Enough! No more of this insane talk, please! I have no idea what you're on about. I have never met you before in my life. And I would certainly remember if I had,' she added, with a look of distaste at G-Mamma's lurid outfit. 'Please, just let us out here – we'll get a taxi the rest of the way. To the police station.'

G-Mamma's face crumpled. 'Oh, this is terrible, Gina! Gina Bellarina! Do you really not remember me? Or anything about your life before all this? Solomon's sizzling sausages! I never thought he'd wipe everything from your memory banks! So that's why you haven't given Janey any Spylet training!'

Janey sighed. This had been the weirdest day of her life, and suddenly she felt incredibly tired. She longed to go home, eat beans on toast and sit with her mum watching something very boring on the television. *Antiques Roadshow* sounded good. 'I told you, G-Mamma. I said you'd made a mistake. My mum is just plain Jean Brown. And I'm just plain old Janey Brown.'

Stamping a black wellington boot on the brake, G-Mamma screeched the car to a halt and turned to the pair in the back.

'Oh no, you are not!' she hissed. 'There is nothing plain about either of you. And since you are severely uneducated, I'm going to have to be some amazing SPI:KE. Let me tell you something, Janey: your mother is Gina Bellarina, and she is the best there has ever been. Well, until now.'

Janey swallowed hard. 'What do you mean, "until now"?'

'Because until now,' explained G-Mamma carefully, 'it seems you really have been just plain old Janey Brown. But under my direction, honey, you are going to grow and grow. You will be what your parents have not allowed you to be. It's in your past. And it's in your future. There's a whole new part of you just waiting to burst out. From now on, my dear godchild, you are Jane Blonde, Sensational Spylet. Welcome to our world.'

5 g-mamma tells all

Jean Brown sniffed. 'Sugar?'

'Four, please,' replied G-Mamma, leaning against the work-surface so the mugs nearly disappeared under her billowing bosom. Janey's mother pointedly moved the cups and nodded towards the chair next to Janey.

'Why don't you sit down? And after we've had a nice calming cup of tea, I can call the hospital for you, if you know which one you came from.'

Shaking her head, G-Mamma meandered across the kitchen and lowered herself on to a seat at the small breakfast table. 'I don't know what I'm going to have to do to get you to believe me, Gina baby!' Her large mascaraed eyes looked close to tears.

Janey watched her mother's expression harden as she slapped a mug of tea down before G-Mamma. 'I don't have time for this, Gee M . . . Gee . . . whatever your name is. Janey and I have both had a terrible day. Strange men come to my home telling me my brother has had an accident and is asking for me; then they string me up with Christmas decorations when I go to find him. These lunatics then try to convince me that they are some kind of super-villains and that my brother-in-law, who I've never even *met*, is involved in some kind of dodgy dealing to do with spies and goodness knows what. And then some mad woman dressed like a circus act forces my lovely only daughter to shinny up the side of an eight-storey building. In fact, what am I doing even talking to you? I'm calling the police . . .'

Janey loved her mum when she was like this. She was usually fairly quiet and unassuming, getting on with her jobs and caring for Janey in an unremarkable way, but she could turn on this icy logic to get her own way. Even the way Jean Brown was holding her mug of tea, while her other hand rested protectively on Janey's shoulder, looked mildly threatening.

'Now come on, Gina,' interrupted G-Mamma. 'What kind of story is that for the police? Fairy lights and super-villains! Even I think it sounds nuts.'

Janey couldn't help admiring G-Mamma's tactics. She obviously wasn't perturbed by Mrs Brown's threats to call the police, in much the same way as she had taken no notice when Janey's mum had insisted on getting out of the car. G-Mamma had simply sped to the Brown's front door with a taloned finger firmly on the central-locking button. She'd then invited herself in on the pretext of checking the house for unwanted visitors, loitering in Janey's room and conducting an overlong search of its darkest recesses.

Slurping noisily at her tea, G-Mamma nodded

towards Janey. 'You just have to let me tell this poor child what she is and how I'm going to help her.'

'And then you'll go?' asked Mrs Brown.

'For the time being, yes.'

Janey's mum sighed. 'Well, I can't believe I'm actually going along with this. At least do me the courtesy of making it short.'

With her chin in her hands, Janey looked from one adult to the other. She really just wanted to get on with her homework and feel normal again. But she had the oddest feeling that, after today, life would never be normal again. And tired as she was, Janey couldn't help noticing a little lift in her stomach, as if her insides were smiling.

G-Mamma beamed cheerily. 'So, Janey, let me tell you who your mother is, when she's not pretending to be Mrs Suburbia, and who your dear, dear father was.' She ignored Mrs Brown's tuts and sighs. 'Your mother is . . . was . . . Gina Bellarina. An international SPI. The best. The most beautiful. The sharpest knife in the drawer. She comes from a long line of female spies that is said to include Mata Hari herself.'

Janey tried not to look at her mother, who was making little circles near her temple with her index finger.

'And what about my . . . my dad?'

'What do you know about him, Janey?' asked G-Mamma gently.

Swallowing hard, Janey looked down at the table. 'His name was Boz Brown. He was a scientist, but he got killed in an explosion after an experiment went wrong, just before I was born. His friend Reggie Baron died too. I don't know what Dad looked like – after the explosion his house burned down and all the family photos were destroyed. But I bet he was really, really handsome.'

G-Mamma's eyes misted over and she stared with an odd mixture of disbelief and compassion at Janey's mum. 'He certainly was, child. Only the most handsome would do for Gina Bellarina. And the most brilliant. That was his real name, you know. Boris Brilliance Brown. Nearly every member of his family, right down from the wonderful Capability Brown, has been a creative genius of some kind – scientists, architects, writers, philosophers.'

'Or really clever businessmen, like Uncle Solomon!' exclaimed Janey.

'Exactly, Blonde-girl,' said G-Mamma with a smile. 'I've never had the great pleasure of meeting your uncle face to face, but I do know he's a genius. He heads up the Solomon's Polificational Investigations network I mentioned before.'

'Polificational?' Janey asked.

'Political, scientific and educational. All at once! He runs the SPI organization without ever revealing himself, so the SPIs who work for him aren't in any more danger than necessary. He works on projects that only a handful of people in the government know about. And he's kind and generous and gives ice lollies to hot children! Although the Sol's Lols business is just a cover, of course.'

'He's never sent me ice lollies, but I have had some presents from him,' agreed Janey.

G-Mamma's eyes lit up. 'Solomon has sent you things? Have you kept them? We'll have to check them all out later. Bound to be a few SPI-buys in there!' She saw Janey's face screw up in confusion. 'SPI-buys are gadgets, girly-girl. You'll see.'

'No, *I'll* see!' cut in Mrs Brown.

'G-Mamma, tell me more about my dad,' said Janey, glaring at her mum. She wasn't going to lose this opportunity to talk to someone who had actually known her father.

'Well, your uncle Solomon is brilliant, as I've said. But your father was perhaps even more brilliant. Solomon was so proud of his brother that he wanted to carry on his work after Boz died. Your dad was a great, great scientist. You knew that already. But he was much more besides. Like your mother here, he was a SPI. A mighty SPI. The best! The perfect match for Gina the Great.'

At this Jean Brown threw her hands in the air, still clutching her mug. Slops of cold tea splashed down her blouse. 'This is insane. Stop it at once. I'm starting to throw drinks down myself, when what I actually want to do is throw them at you. I'm going to change my top, and when I'm back down in one minute I want you out of here. And then I want to forget this whole ridiculous day.'

G-Mamma nodded resignedly. But the second Mrs Brown had left the room, she reached over and grabbed Janey's hands. 'She doesn't believe it because her brain's been fried!'

'You really think her memory's been wiped?' gulped Janey.

'Yep. Solomon did it himself. And I think I know why: to protect you, Janey. To give you a chance at a normal, happy life. That would never have happened if your mum had continued her SPI work. So Gina's memory was meddled with – but I never knew until now that she'd been completely wiped.'

'She does say she can't remember much about my dad other than that she really loved him,' said Janey quietly. 'But I thought that was just an excuse so she didn't have to talk about him. Maybe you're right.'

'I am, Janey. And know this, Jane Blonde: you are the daughter of two of the greatest SPIs the world has ever known. Your genes are Out Of Sight. Impeccable. We could only begin to imagine what the combination of Gina Bellarina and Boris Brilliance Brown could have produced. Well, we don't need to imagine any more. Here you are. And here I am, at last. I've always been your godmother, Janey – watching from a distance to make sure nothing happened to you. And Sol's Sticky Lols, your life's been pretty dull so far, I have to say! But now things are hotting up, mighty all-righty. Solomon has made a discovery so huge that he's not sure who he can trust. He has already been betrayed by someone inside his closest circle, which is exactly why the Sinerlesse Group are after him. The double-crosser tipped them off, told them that Solomon is hiding a big, big secret. They'll do anything to get hold of it. They're motivated by pure greed and evil, Janey, which makes them very dangerous indeed. You saw today what they're capable of. Anyway, Solomon has had to go into hiding to protect what he knows, but just before he disappeared, he sent you a message – and he sent me here to be your SPI:KE.'

Janey could hear her mother on the landing above but was completely transfixed. She needed to know more. 'My "spike"?'

'S.P.I.K.E, Janey. Solomon's Polifications Investigations: Kid Educator. You're a Spylet now, a SPI-in-training. I'm going to teach you how to be an amazing spy. And I'll look after you too, as much as I can.'

'But tell me about my uncle Solomon's secret. Why has he sent me a message? Who is Jane Blonde? Tell me—'

'I'm coming,' shouted Jean Brown down the stairs in a hide-and-seek voice.

G-Mamma pinched the sallow cheeks on either side of Janey's wide-open mouth. 'No time now, girly. I'll be back for you soon. Look after your mother.'

And with surprising grace for a woman of her girth, G-Mamma flitted from the room and out into the darkness.

That night, after Janey had lain awake for hours, her mind turning over every detail of what had happened that day, she swallowed her pride and crept to her mother's room. The bedside light was still on and her mum was lying flat on her back, staring at the ceiling. She propped herself up on one elbow.

'You can't sleep either?'

'I keep thinking about everything G-Mamma said.'

Mrs Brown sniffed. 'I keep thinking about your dad too. I wish I could remember him better.'

Janey nodded. 'Me too, Mum. And what about Uncle Solomon? Why it is you never got to meet him? Wasn't he even at your wedding?'

'I honestly don't remember, Janey.' With an almighty heave of her shoulders that made the duvet rise and fall, Janey's mum let out a sigh. 'The wedding is so blurry. But I think your Uncle Sol was a foreign aid worker in Ethiopia when I married your dad. He couldn't just drop everything and rush back. And then, when your dad was killed . . . I've tried, Janey. Over the years, I really have tried to make contact with Solomon. I just don't think he's interested in being tied to the past. He sends you the odd present, yes. But I expect he's not really used to children and families and doesn't quite know what to make of it all. I'm so sorry.'

Janey smiled as her mum dropped a kiss on to her forehead. 'That's OK, Mum. I feel better now we've talked about it. I'll go back to my room now.'

'All right, darling.' Her mother yawned, clearly feeling better too. 'Goodnight.'

Janey scampered back to her room. Her mum's words certainly had made her feel much better, because they'd reminded her of something G-Mamma had said. Ferreting under her bed, Janey hauled out a battered cardboard box which had held her very first school shoes.

'Bingo!'

As she removed the lid, her eyes fell upon the few precious but pretty ordinary gifts Uncle Solomon had sent her over the years. There was a bottle of perfume that her mother had squirted over the pair of them, before babbling on about how it was much too old for Janey, and howling with laughter at just how silly men like Sol could be. Janey had nearly had to chuck cold water over her mum, she'd gone on and on for so long. The next year Uncle Solomon had done better, sending Janey a set of glittery hairslides shaped like rocketships. Then there was a pencil case, shaped like a very large pencil, which had a fat, slug-shaped pen inside. The most recent present was a short metal ruler. Janey couldn't imagine how these gifts could be useful for SPI work, but if G-Mamma was for real – and Janey was starting to believe she was – then perhaps the presents *were* gadgets!

Janey's favourite gift from her uncle had arrived when she was very small. It was her first-ever book of dingbats and puzzles. Janey now pulled it out from beneath all the other gifts and spread it open on her lap.

'"Top heavy!"' she shouted excitedly at a picture of a box with the word 'heavy' floating just below the highest line. '"Fading away! . . . Get around to it!" What's this one . . . ? Oh, I know – "It's a small world"!'

As she gazed at the tiny word 'world' on the page, it dawned on her that it was Uncle Solomon who had sparked off her addiction for solving puzzles. Maybe that made more sense now, if what G-Mamma said was true.

Perhaps he'd sort of been training her, without anyone even realizing. Janey looked at the dingbat that Uncle Solomon had created himself on the inside cover of the book. It was written in unusual bronze ink.

It was the only dingbat that Janey had never been able to work out. Lots of Us? Many of U? And the little pony – what did that mean? Had Uncle Sol been trying to tell her something? Janey wanted more than anything to believe what G-Mamma had told her – that her uncle was trying to get a message to her. That she, Janey Brown, could be about to embark on something truly important.

'The letter!' Janey cried as she suddenly remembered it. 'Uncle Sol's letter!'

Grabbing her presents, Janey crept downstairs to the kitchen. Her school bag was still under the table, where she'd kicked it when they came in earlier with G-Mamma. Janey flicked on the kitchen light and delved between her homework books. Nothing. She picked the books up and shook each one upside down, like she did with birthday cards in the hope that some money would drop out. This time, though, she was looking for something much, much more important than money.

Hadn't she, that very morning, received a letter from Uncle Solomon? A message from her uncle, just as G-Mamma had said.

And now it was gone.

Janey felt a hot, angry surge of indignation in her veins. The old Janey would have been upset that she'd lost a prized letter from one of her only relatives. After she had sobbed a little and sulked a little more, she would have got over it. But since G-Mamma had turned up at the school gates, Janey Brown was starting to feel a whole lot stronger. She'd seen those Sinerlesse men up on the roof with her very own eyes, and she'd helped her mum escape. Something deadly serious was happening to her and there were two people that Janey had to rely on now: G-Mamma – and herself. 'I don't know who's got that letter, or where it is,' Janey promised her pencil case as she shoved it into her bag, 'but I'm getting it back. Tomorrow people are going to see a different side to Janey Brown.'

binned

Once she got to school, the conviction and strength Janey had felt the previous night dripped out of her like water from a leaky tap. She had massive plasters on her knees, and her face was a cyclone of colours from socking herself in the eye during the tussle with the postman. The Cool Police would have every right to nee-naw up to her and spirit her away. Head down, she scanned the ground for her letter. Had someone stolen it? No. She must have lost it somewhere. Dejected, she trudged past the crowds of happy schoolchildren and made her way straight into the classroom. The sooner she got those legs under a desk the better.

Janey was sitting quietly, wondering how she was supposed to contact G-Mamma about the letter from Uncle Sol, when she realized with a shock that someone was in the room with her. She looked up to see her teacher, Miss Rale.

'Oh, Janey! I didn't think anyone was in here! Why aren't you out enjoying the sunshine before you get stuck in here all day?'

'I wanted some time to think, miss. It's all right, isn't it?'

The teacher walked to Janey's desk and bent down beside it. 'Well, it's not really allowed, Janey, but seeing as it's you I won't say anything. Just don't make a habit of it. What was it you wanted to think about? Can I help?'

Hesitating, Janey looked at Miss Rale. The young woman's eyes were round and expectant. She looked so kind and understanding that Janey suddenly felt like telling her everything.

'It all sounds a bit mad, miss,' she started.

'Don't worry. You can tell me anything you like, Janey.'

Janey felt as though she was bursting with the enormity of her secret. Her mum had been brain-wiped, so she thought it was all invented, and Janey had no friends to talk it through with. Even G-Mamma had disappeared without telling Janey how she could contact her. More than anything, Janey wanted someone to talk to.

'Well, the thing is, yesterday . . .'

But just as she was about to blurt everything out, the other pupils, led by Alfie, coursed into the classroom, chattering loudly and slamming desks. Sighing, Miss Rale leaned forward and whispered in Janey's ear, 'Come and talk to me later, when it's a bit quieter.'

She patted Janey's hand and walked back to the front of the room, calling for the class to calm down. Nearly all of them tucked their bags under the desk or grabbed their pencils or turned to face the front. Only Alfie Halliday seemed to have noticed that Janey and the teacher had been chatting, and he scowled at her with such aggression that Janey blinked in surprise. But soon anything other than school matters was pushed out of the way until lunchtime.

Janey picked up her lunchbox. Ketchup sarnies, no doubt. As she pushed her way through to claim her normal lonely spot at the back of the dining hall, Janey felt a hand on her arm.

'You and teacher were looking very cosy there, Brown!' said Alfie casually.

Janey shrugged. 'She just wanted to know how I was settling in.'

'Oh?' muttered Alfie. 'And what did you tell her?'

Janey felt a little surge of heat in her chest and for once looked Alfie straight in the face. 'I . . . I told her the other pupils are awful, and nobody's friendly like at my last school. I told her about the nasty notes. And . . . and I said I thought it was probably you writing them!'

Alfie's jaw dropped. 'Me? Why would I do that? You're nuts, Brown.'

'Well, who is it then?' Janey tried to glare back at him even though she could feel tears gathering behind her eyes.

Alfie shook his head. 'I dunno. You should forget it. Why don't you just chuck the notes in the rubbish if they bother you so much?'

'I'm going to have my lunch,' said Janey abruptly. She shoved past Alfie and ran out of the hall, her face hot with embarrassment. She needed some fresh air.

And besides, something Alfie had said had made her think.

If she'd dropped the letter in the playground yesterday then it might have blown away. But there was a good chance that the cleaners would have swept it up at the end of the day and put it into the rubbish bins.

Looking round to check that nobody was paying her any attention, Janey made her way furtively around the edge of the school building until she reached the four massive steel bins at the back of the kitchens. She found two old paint tins nearby and stacked them one on top of the other, then stepped gingerly on to the top, clinging to the edge of the nearest bin to steady herself.

The stench was disgusting: festering school dinners mingled with rotting grass from the recently mown playing field. Reaching out a hand, Janey steeled herself to move aside a small quagmire of disintegrating sprouts. It looked like a cowpat, and smelt even worse.

'Gross. Even my sandwiches are better than that!' Janey held her nose and was just about to plunge her hand into the revolting bin when a wonderful thought occurred to her. She was looking for a letter, an envelope. Envelopes were made of paper, and paper went into a different bin, ready for recycling. Lucky I go to such a 'green' school, thought Janey.

She moved her paint-can stepladder round to all the other bins until she found the paper one, hoisted herself over the edge and slithered head first into an avalanche of paper. She felt completely ridiculous. Anyone in a helicopter would be able to see her underwear. In fact, that's all they'd see – a set of knobbly, wriggling knees and her faded pink knickers bearing a motif saying 'Thanks for Thursdays!'.

Not even the right day, Janey thought, trying to right herself. Should be my 'Wonderful Wednesdays!' ones. Good job there's nobody here!

Just then the bin swayed, and her heart crashed. There *was* somebody there! Janey slithered down to the bottom, trying to find something to hang on to, but the paper came away in her hands as she grabbed at the metal sides. Then the bin tipped and swung back with such violence that the next thing Janey knew, she was lying on the gravel in a landslide of paper, with a small, angry face glowering at her.

'What do you think you're doing in my bin?' yelled the face.

'Wh-wha . . .' Janey sat up and the face came into focus. It was the boy she'd bumped into the day before. The slight, delicate features and the cropped, ice-white hair were instantly recognizable. He was wearing his too-short grey trousers again, with a matching jumper and a St Earl's school badge.

'You heard! What are you doing in my bin?' the boy squeaked, shoving his nose closer to Janey's. He cleared his throat quickly.

'*Your* bin?'

'Yeah,' the boy continued gruffly. 'My family's in charge of all the cleaning here, and I do the bins in my lunch hour. Nobody messes with my bins, OK?'

Janey held back a smile. 'It's OK, I understand. My mum's a cleaner too.'

The boy's lip curled, displaying small, even, ice-white teeth. 'Yeah. I worked that out for myself. Your mum works for my sister.'

'I . . . Does she?' stammered Janey. 'What's your name?'

'Freddie. Freddie Lear. My family owns the company your mum works for – St Earl's Sanitation and Security Enterprises. Miss Lear – your mum's boss – she's my sister.

'Oh right. My mum's mentioned her. I'm Janey. Nice to meet you.'

'Course it is. So I suppose you're grovelling around in my bin for a reason. Looking for this?'

Janey stared in amazement as Freddie held up her letter from Uncle Solomon. 'That's mine!'

'That's what I said.' Freddie handed Janey the envelope. 'Found it when I was sorting the bins earlier. Looks like it got a bit slimy in all that muck.'

'Thanks!' Janey stared at the slightly gooey envelope and then back at Freddie, who had thrust his hands into his pockets. He shrugged.

'S'all right. See ya.'

Freddie leaped on to a small silver bike leaning against one of the other bins and rode away without a backwards glance. Getting to her feet, Janey discovered that she was now covered in glue and clumps of old glitter. There was also a nasty aroma of damp paper clinging to her, but she couldn't care less. She'd found what she was looking for! Pushing her uncle's letter inside her jumper, Janey scudded around the building back towards the main doors of the school.

Unfortunately the Class Superstar and his crew were just inside. Wrinkling his nose, Alfie cocked his head to one side. 'Why were you meeting that weirdo at the bins, Brown? Boyfriend, is he?'

'I . . . I had to get something. Freddie was helping me. He works in the bins.'

'Hmm. Freddie Lear – Bin Boy. His family must be so proud of him,' said Alfie. 'I hope whatever you wanted was worth smelling like a tramp for the rest of the day.'

Alfie looked with interest at her empty hands. Quickly Janey slapped her hand against her stomach, but she was not fast enough. With lightning reactions, Alfie stepped across, pulled up the bottom of her jumper and yanked the envelope out of its hiding place.

'Oh, a love letter. From Lear? No wonder you had to get it back. Let's see, shall we?'

Alfie ripped across the top of the envelope, twitching it out of the way as Janey tried to grab it back. His fingers pulled out a single sheet of paper, and he gazed at it for a moment before letting out a short laugh.

'Well, that's great. A picture of a frog.'

Alfie handed the piece of paper back to Janey.

She looked down at it, her heart beating heavily. Janey turned it over and scanned the edges, holding it up to the light, searching for some writing. But Alfie was right. It was just a plain, dumb picture – a simple line drawing of a rather bored and insignificant-looking frog.

Just then Miss Rale called to them to start making their way back to the classroom. Janey put the frog picture back in her bag and walked slowly along behind Alfie and his gang. She wondered how she would get through the afternoon, reeking of bins and aching with disappointment.

becoming blonde

'I did tell you, Janey,' said her mother gently. 'I don't think Solomon knows very much about girls. Not that a boy would find a bad drawing of a frog interesting . . . I bet Uncle Solomon's never even heard of most of the things you're into.'

After showing her mum the picture, Janey had hidden the gooey envelope under her mattress so she could study the frog later. Now she was in her dressing gown, while her school clothes flipped over and over in the washing machine being purged of their smelly, slimy bits.

Janey sighed. 'He sent me good presents before!'

'Well, yes, but maybe that was just luck,' her mother continued. 'Can we just agree that Uncle Solomon is likely to be a huge disappointment, and leave it at that?'

'I was very disappointed today,' admitted Janey. 'I don't know what I expected,' she went on, 'but I thought he might at least have something to *say*. I mean—'

Janey was interrupted by the doorbell. On the way to the front door, her mother hugged her. 'Let me just get this and we can sit and have a natter.'

Janey took a sip of her hot chocolate, but almost spat it out again when she heard her mother's sharp voice.

'You can't seriously want *more*!'

Footsteps clattered down the hallway into the kitchen, and Janey looked up to see her mother standing there with G-Mamma.

'Hi, honey-child!' beamed G-Mamma. 'I just popped round to ask your lovely – well, formerly lovely – mother if I could borrow some sugar.'

With a decided air of discontent Mrs Brown foraged in a cupboard. Finally, she thrust an unopened bag of granulated at G-Mamma.

'There. Even you should be able to keep going on that for a few days. Though why you had to come all the way over here just to get sugar, I do not know.'

G-Mamma's thin, arched eyebrows rose towards her curls. 'But I thought that's what neighbours did?'

'Neighbours?' shouted Janey and her mother at the same time.

Beaming, G-Mamma stretched out her hand to Janey. 'Yes indeedy, Blonde-girl. I am your new next-door neighbour. Bought the house from the lovely Mr Harris just last night.'

'But . . . but . . .' stammered Mrs Brown. 'But that's impossible! You can't have! And even if you did buy the house, you couldn't possibly have exchanged contracts and signed everything and moved in within twenty-four hours!'

'Have you really moved in next door?' asked Janey incredulously.

G-Mamma polished her nails against her bosom with a pleased smile. 'Yep. My very influential friends in the government sorted it out for me.'

'Just like that?' scoffed Janey's mum.

'Yep, just like that. And if you could remember anything about your past, Gina Bellarina, you could be sorted out just like that as well.'

As Mrs Brown started to snarl like a slavering bulldog, Janey hissed at G-Mamma, 'Perhaps you'd better go now. Maybe we could talk tomorrow.'

Grinning secretively, G-Mamma inclined her head into her layered neck, turtle-like, and stepped back into the hall. 'We'll see about that, Janey baby. Bye, Gina.' And she stalked proudly from the house, turned right directly past the front window and stepped through a gate in the fence to her new home.

Mrs Brown slumped into a chair. 'What have we done to deserve all this, Janey?'

'I . . . I think perhaps she's just lonely, Mum.'

'Hmm. Well, she shouldn't just inflict herself on the first people she comes across.' But Janey could tell from the softer tone of her mother's voice that she felt a slight twinge of sympathy.

Janey kissed her mother's cheek. She couldn't help wondering why her mum was so quick to dismiss everything that G-Mamma had told them. But she knew it would be a whole lot easier if she pretended to go along with her. Right now she needed some time alone to think about what was happening.

Janey forced out a yawn. 'Well, she'll probably get bored and leave us alone soon, Mum. Let's just ignore her.' She yawned again. 'Oh, is that the time? I'm exhausted. Feel a bit bashed and bruised after the last couple of days. Bedtime for me!'

More than a little shocked that Janey was rushing to bed of her own accord, Mrs Brown blew her daughter a kiss. 'OK then. Goodnight, darling.'

Janey twisted herself awkwardly under the duvet, trying to avoid scraping her sore knees or leaning on her bruised wrist. She really was exhausted. Clutching the frog picture she had rescued from beneath her mattress, she started to fall asleep. But moments later she was sitting up, trying to work out where a loud, insistent tapping was coming from. It had a metallic ring to it, like the sound of a horseshoe being hammered out on a blacksmith's anvil. Reluctantly, Janey eased herself out of bed and made her way towards the source of the sound.

It was coming from her fireplace. She flicked on her bedside light and approached the black iron grate where she knelt down on her sore knees. Suddenly the tapping stopped and a familiar voice bounced into the room.

'Turn off the light, Spylet!'

Janey ignored how silly she was feeling and spoke into the grate. 'G-Mamma? What are you doing in my fireplace?'

'I'm not in your fireplace, Blonde-girl! I'm in my

fireplace! You'll have to turn off the light – don't want your mum checking to see you're in Noddy Bye-bye Land and finding you gone. Then you can come through.'

'Come through?' Janey switched the lamp off and stumbled back to the fireplace. 'Right. What do I do now?'

'Just come on down, child! Bring it on!'

A sliver of light appeared at the very bottom of the iron panel that lined the back of the fireplace. Janey watched as the glimmer broadened until it was ten, then twenty, then thirty centimetres high. Now she could make out G-Mamma's fluffy scarlet mules on the other side. Noiselessly the panel continued to rise, until Janey could see up to G-Mamma's waist. It stopped abruptly and G-Mamma's rosy cheeks suddenly popped into view.

'Well, come on, zany Janey. What are you waiting for?'

Still holding the curled-up frog picture, Janey shuffled on hands and knees through the short tunnel between her room and G-Mamma's.

From out of nowhere a streak of fur shot past her face.

'Aaaaaaargh! What was that?' yelled Janey.

'Whatty-what?'

'Some animal! A furry snake-thing!'

G-Mamma tutted impatiently and dragged Janey through the fireplace. 'It's a kitten, Blonde. Calm down. Can't have our ace Spylet frightened by a widdle puddy cat, can we?' She helped Janey to her feet, then pressed her palm flat against the wall. The iron panel slid shut.

'Welcome to my SPI-lab. You've got the same control panel on your side. I think I'll get them to widen it though, so you can just step through instead of scrabbling around like a chimney sweep.'

Janey didn't reply. She was too busy gawping at the room that lay before her. The kitten had disappeared, but there was still plenty to look at.

Every single wall on the top floor of G-Mamma's house had been knocked through. The surfaces were either white enamel or surgical steel, as gleaming and clinical as an operating theatre. Enormous floor-to-ceiling cupboards lined the walls, and nearly every one had a glass front, through which Janey could see a vast array of equipment, from scissors and nail files to jet skis and backpack propeller sets. One cupboard had a shining steel door and another boasted a curved white front with magnetic pictures and letters stuck on it – Janey guessed that this was G-Mamma's fridge. In the middle of the huge expanse of floor were three sleek stainless-steel islands. One had nothing on it at all; one was covered in an array of test tubes, Bunsen burners and bubbling bottles, like something out of a Frankenstein movie; and the third was home to G-Mamma's massive collection of make-up and a series of mirrors with which to view her face from any angle.

'Amazing!' was all Janey could say. How had G-Mamma got all this done so quickly?

G-Mamma opened the cupboard with the metal door. 'Wish I could say the same for you, honey-mine.

You are the most bumped and filthy Spylet I have seen in a long, long time. Into the Wower with you.'

'Er, do you mean the shower?'

'No, I said exactly what I mean. A SPI shower is called a Wower.' G-Mamma grinned. 'You'll see why in a moment. Go on, you need all the help you can get.'

Looking down at herself, Janey could see that G-Mamma was right. And before she could hesitate, she was shoved into the shower room, fully clothed. The steel door slammed shut.

Janey looked around. 'Where's the shower then?'

She was enclosed in a small cubicle made up entirely of shimmering surfaces. She caught sight of her reflection in one and giggled. No longer lean and gangly, the girl peering back at her was no bigger than a toddler, with babyish creases in her chubby knees and elbows. In the next mirror she looked fantastically tall, stretching to the very top of the glass with a worm-wide, spaghetti body. To her right, her reflection was wide and soft, with pudgy arms that would have made a teddy bear proud.

'G-Mamma!' she shouted again. 'What do I do? There's no shower in here!'

'No shower?' G-Mamma's voice boomed into the cubicle. There was clearly some kind of public-address system. 'Course there is. Just say, "Wow me," and get on out here, will you? Zippety split, Janey!'

'Er, OK.' Feeling very silly, Janey closed her eyes. 'Um, please, er, Wow me!'

There was a tiny click, like a camera shutter.

Suddenly the whole cubicle began to fill with steam. Damp, glistening air surrounded her, heavy with pearly moisture. Miraculously, it seemed to Janey that the tiny droplets of water were soothing her cuts and bruises so she no longer felt any pain, and instead of her nightclothes feeling sodden and heavy, she was encased in silk, or something even lighter, like gossamer. It was like being enclosed inside a snow-globe, with glittering flakes swirling and whirling around her.

Janey's head spun slightly as a pair of robot hands reached from the back of the cubicle and moved towards her. A moment later all the nerve-endings in her scalp tingled as her whole head was pummelled and cleaned by the metal fingers, and her hair was massaged with a sweet-smelling potion. Next she felt the hands at work on her fingers and toes, polishing her nails to perfection. Then suddenly she was being blasted with warm air while a third hand reached for her face.

'Right! That's enough! Come on out now!'

Stepping from the cubicle, Janey was immediately swept up in a huge embrace by G-Mamma.

'Oh, look at you!' crowed G-Mamma. 'What a Spylet! Second rule of SPI work, Blonde-girl: be sensational!' G-Mamma swung Janey round and pushed her towards the polished steel of the Wower door.

Janey gasped at her reflection. She could no longer see her savaged, scrawny joints or her bruised and bloodied fingers. In fact, she couldn't see any of her skin below her neck, as she was now encased in a silver Lycra catsuit that seemed to iron out her angular bones and give her smooth curves instead. She looked like an Olympic gymnast from the twenty-second century. And now Janey could see what those robotic hands had been doing to her – in place of her limp, mousy hair was a high, sleek ponytail of platinum blonde. Suddenly her cheekbones sprang to attention and her lips looked plump and rosy. And her vision was definitely sharper. Janey wondered if that had anything to do with the slender black glasses from behind which her grey, long-lashed eyes now sparkled.

'Wow!' she said. 'I look like a pop star!'

G-Mamma grinned back proudly, as though the transformation had been entirely her work. 'For the first time in your life you look like what you are meant to be: Jane Blonde, Sensational Spylet.'

Swelling with joy, Janey looked herself up and down. She nodded. 'I do. I feel different, G-Mamma. I really think I could be something . . . something special!'

But G-Mamma was pulling at the stretchy silver catsuit and pinging it back against Janey's skin. 'OK. It's not all about looking good. SPI-suit: heat and fire resistant, aerodynamic, waterproof (obviously), withstands certain pressures and weights but not all. You could be crushed but not melted. Fleet-feet pads on your soles – you can run at speeds of up to thirty miles an hour and also be propelled off the floor to a maximum height of three metres if you bring both feet down together. Ponytail: can be used as a whip for self-defence, a dagger if frozen solid and, you know, it keeps your hair out of your eyes. Which brings me to the Ultra-gogs, for extra-sharp day vision, night vision, heat detection and information. They may look like specs, but actually they're a voice-activated satellite-sourced search engine. Did you get all that?'

Janey gulped. 'Are you joking?'

'Nope, it's no joke. You've been getting ready for this moment your whole life. You just didn't know it. There's only one Jane Blonde in the world. Only one girl who can wear this outfit – and it's you.'

Janey nodded while G-Mamma continued, looking more than a little stern. 'I am deadly serious, Blonde. And you had better start treating this as deadly serious, because you are in some deadly serious trouble yourself. Understand me, Spylet?'

'Y-yes, G-Mamma. I understand you,' said Janey, even though her mind was whirling in confusion.

'Good.' G-Mamma moved to a computer screen that had risen from the desk and tapped away at it, her long nails clicking on the keyboard.

'Now. I think I ought to get on with briefing you about your uncle, Spylet. Solomon Brown, scientist and SPI. As I said, just before he went underground he sent me instructions – along with his kitty-cat, whom you've already met – to make sure you're well versed in everything Solomon's Polifical Investigations – that's SPI – can do. And why they do it! So here we go: your uncle Solomon's organization is employed by the government to come up with new inventions to assist them in their secret operations. All the gadgets and whatnots you'll come into contact with – no doubt including those presents Solomon sent you – have been invented and used by your wonderful uncle, or indeed by your father before him. Other covert groups have to beg, steal, even kill to get hold of stuff that isn't half as good. Solomon is the master of SPI technology.

'The gadgetry arm gets its commissions from someone in MI5 – we know him only as Copper Knickers. I mean, Copernicus. (Have to be sooooo careful how you say that!) Anyway, the last thing your father was working on was really big. When he died, Solomon said he would take over the project. He's been working on it ever since, and the only person he reports to is old Knickers himself. I mean, Copernicus. We know it's called Project Crystal Clear, but beyond that we don't know much else. We also know the Sinerlesse Group have got a whiff of the secret – so someone close to Solomon has spilled a few beans.'

'So, the Sinerlesse Group. I mean, they know where I live – are they going to come and kill me or something?' asked Janey, turning pale 'What do they want, exactly?'

'Calm down, Blondey. They're not going to kill you. You're too valuable. Now listen. Sinerlesse is another spy organization,' said G-Mamma, typing frantically. 'At one time we were all on the same side. They were the field-operations team who tested our inventions – although at that time they didn't call themselves Sinerlesse. They were just a band of outdoor specialists. But then they broke away, turned rogue – and gave themselves a snaky old name. Anyway, they moved abroad and spied for money, selling secrets to the highest bidder. But now they're back. And they've got a new leader: Ariel. Information has leaked through that this Ariel character is ruthless. That he's motivated by more than money. He wants power. And he thinks that whatever Sol has discovered will give the Sinerlesse Group just that. They've done a really good job of keeping themselves hidden, so we don't know who Ariel is. They've always been clever spies, Blondette. Don't ever underestimate them. They're tricky. And, most of all, they're dangerous.' G-Mamma finished her speech with a deep breath.

'Right.' Janey didn't know what else to say.

'So – be careful.'

'I will.'

G-Mamma looked at her for a moment, then nodded, apparently satisfied that Janey was taking everything in. 'Righty almighty. Now we need to analyse the message Solomon sent you. When did you last hear from him?'

So much had happened that Janey had lost track of what day it was. She struggled hard to think when the letter had arrived. 'Um, Wednesday.'

G-Mamma swivelled back to face her. 'And what did he say?'

'He didn't say anything. He never does. I think you might have the wrong idea about how close we are, G-Mamma. I don't even know him really. I've never even met him. He just sent me a drawing, that's all.'

'OK,' said G-Mamma slowly and with deliberate patience. 'So get the drawing, Spylet!'

Janey positioned herself in front of G-Mamma's shimmering marble fireplace. She was just about to fetch the drawing from her room when something dreadful occurred to her.

'Oh no! I took it in the Wower!'

'What?'

'It was in my hand! I took it into the Wower by accident.'

G-Mamma rolled her eyes, then stepped smartly up to the steel door and rapped on it. A slot appeared, and from it shot a soggy wad of paper. Janey and G-Mamma looked down at it. Only a few traces of the drawing remained, like an impossible dot-to-dot.

'Don't worry, I'll scan it,' muttered G-Mamma, skewering a corner with a fingernail and returning to the computer bench. Janey followed, and watched a glass panel set into the enamel surface flash as it scanned what little information it could find into its processors.

'Ah, look. Something's happening. Yes . . . Yes . . .' G-Mamma pointed to the computer screen. 'The original picture can't be reproduced, but the computer can tell us something about it. Here it comes. Wait for it . . . wait for it.'

And in large, distinct red letters, up popped the word 'FROG'.

'Is that it?' Janey asked after a while. 'I could have told you that.'

'You could?' G-Mamma rubbed a hand across her round, peacock-blue-painted eyes. 'So, Blonde, we have wasted valuable time. We could have been well on the way to tracking down your uncle already. Now, what's the significance of a frog?'

'I don't know,' said Janey a little sulkily.

'Was it a frog-man? A diver?'

'No. It was just a frog.'

'Does your family eat French food? You know, like frogs' legs?'

'Euugh. No way.'

'Well, have any of you got webbed feet like a froggy?'

'No! I don't know! Uncle Sol might have, I've never seen him, but my feet and Mum's are completely normal, thank you very much.'

'Think, Blonde! Solomon's using this to get a message to you. It must be important. You have to work it out!'

Janey's head felt as if it was full of smoke. 'I just don't know what the frog means. If it was a puzzle or a dingbat I could work it out – I'm good at that sort of thing. But this picture doesn't make any sense!' Something ticked in her mind as she spoke. She knew she was missing something – some vital bit of information that would make things clear. But what?

'No, I don't get it at all. I'm too tired, G-Mamma. I have to go to bed.'

'Not like that, you don't!'

G-Mamma grabbed Janey before she could get to the

fireplace and propelled her into the Wower. 'Third rule of SPI work, Janey: decode, debrief, de-Wow.'

'But I like it—'

Janey's protests were cut short as she was flung once more into the glimmering Wower cubicle. G-Mamma had forgotten to turn the microphone off and could now be heard prancing around the SPI-lab, practising her rapping.

> *'Decode, debrief, de-Wow, oh yeah,*
> *And do it all right now, oh yeah,*
> *Decode, debrief, de-Wow, oh yeah,*
> *G-Mamma will show you how. OH YEAH!'*

Janey grinned and danced along a little as the Wower did its work. The reverse transformation was far less soothing and actually slightly uncomfortable as the robot hands put new snags into Janey's hair, scrubbed her face and whipped her Ultra-gogs away. At least her injuries weren't returned to her, as the Wower transformed Jane Blonde back into Janey-Brown-in-PJs and spat her out into the SPI-lab.

Grabbing the remains of her frog picture, Janey crawled into her own bedroom. As the panel closed behind her, she didn't see G-Mamma's eyebrows and mouth curve into a satisfied grin of approval.

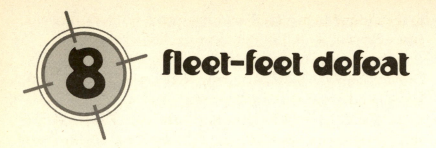

fleet-feet defeat

Ever since the previous night, the feeling that she was missing something important had been thumping around Janey's brain like a sock in a tumble dryer. It was impossible to concentrate, and Miss Rale noticed that Janey was unusually distracted. The teacher made her way over to Janey's desk.

'Janey, I can see something is on your mind. Why don't you come and see me this lunchtime?'

'No, I'm fine, Miss Rale, but thanks.'

The teacher smiled, pointing at Janey's blank exercise book. 'OK. Well then, you'd better start your essay.'

Janey grinned back guiltily, then reached for something to write with. Her fingers brushed against something unfamiliar in her bag. It was the pencil case Uncle Solomon had sent.

Alfie Halliday leaned across the aisle between their desks. 'Boring topic, huh? What I want to be when I grow up. Dull, dull, dull.'

'Oh, and I suppose you think it should suit me down

to the ground then?' said Janey, glaring at him. 'Boring old Janey Brown! Well, I'm not like that. OK?'

For a long moment Alfie stared at her. 'Chill out, Brown. You'd better learn how to keep your cool, you know. And I told you, I didn't write those notes.'

Pulling the chubby pen out of the pencil case, Janey shrugged. Alfie was right, it was a boring essay. And anyway, who would believe her if she wrote that she was going to be a spy? Like her parents. The class would die of laughter! She would have to make up something ordinary.

Pen poised, Janey tried to copy the title neatly on to the page. It remained blank. Sighing, she tried again, but no matter how hard she pressed down, no ink came out of Uncle Solomon's pen. Great. A present that didn't even work. Janey was just about to throw it back in the pencil case when she noticed another, narrower nib at the other end of the pen. Turning the pen upside down, she pressed the new nib on to the paper, ready to start.

Liquid, clear as tears, spilled out of the narrow nib and across the paper. Janey watched as the words she had tried to write appeared, illuminated one by one as the watery substance touched them. There was the title, bright as daylight: 'What I'm going to be'.

Janey's mouth fell open. The pen held invisible ink and its antidote! It was probably a really common gadget, but Janey couldn't wait to get home and try it out on the frog picture. Maybe there was a hidden message written on it.

When the bell rang at noon, Janey did something she would never have considered before, because it wasn't allowed – she went home for lunch. Feeling naughty, but more than a little excited, she picked the lock of the front door with a hairgrip, just as G-Mamma had shown her. Once inside, she fetched the now dry frog picture from under her mattress and sat at the kitchen table, grabbing the pencil case from her bag. She pointed the smaller nib at the drawing, took a deep breath and pressed down hard.

The same clear liquid appeared, flowing from the pen across the page. Janey could hardly stop herself from shouting out – words were appearing, scribbled at an angle across the top of the page.

Hi Brenda, cld you put this in ENVELOPE & send to Janey? Thx, Sol.

Janey felt sick with disappointment. A hastily scrawled instruction from her uncle to his secretary was all she'd revealed. It was so innocent that Janey wondered why her uncle had bothered to write it in invisible ink. Perhaps he just liked to keep his secretary on her toes. She pressed and squirted all over the paper, but no other words appeared.

'That can't be it!' she said.

Just then Janey heard footsteps outside on the path. She dashed to the front door and peeked through the letter box. Her mum's shoes were approaching, followed by another pair of sensible brown pumps. Janey squeaked — if her mum found her here she would be grounded forever, and no amount of SPI-buys or G-Mammas could ever save her.

Janey pelted up the stairs just as the front door opened. She took the last few steps two at a time and managed to roll on to the landing just as her mother and her guest started taking their coats off.

'Nice of you to pop round, Miss Lear. Can I get you some tea?' asked Mrs Brown.

Janey crawled, quiet as a mouse, into her bedroom and over to the fireplace. She tapped the wall, and the entrance to G-Mamma's place began to open. Janey hurled herself into G-Mamma's SPI-lab, calling out to her SPI:KE, 'G-Mamma! Are you here? G-Mamma!'

The only answer was a loud miaow from G-Mamma's kitten, who was hiding somewhere, nowhere to be seen. Janey was just about to make her way to the spiral staircase in the far corner of the lab when she spotted something on the countertop. It was a pair of foot-shaped pads with thick treads, like the soles of trainers. Fleet-feet! Glancing at her watch, Janey could see that she had only a couple of minutes to get back to her classroom before afternoon registration. School was a good ten minutes away, even if she ran. She paused for just a moment before reaching a decision. Surely G-Mamma wouldn't mind if she used the Fleet-feet for such a good cause? Holding the Fleet-feet against the soles of her black patent school shoes, left first and then right,

Janey watched with amazement as the pads moulded themselves to the right size and shape, then swiftly became invisible. Her shoes looked no different from the way they had a moment ago, but Janey could feel a buzzing pins-and-needles sensation fizzing up through her feet and into her ankles. She skipped down the stairs, located G-Mamma's front door and let herself out into the street.

From the end of the road, Janey started to run. The feeling was incredible. Her tingling feet flew across the pavement, making her leap along in powerful, smooth strides that took her over three or four paving stones at a time. Realizing that she would draw attention to herself if she ran along the main road to school, Janey switched course and pelted along the quieter streets. Almost laughing aloud with the delight of being able to bound, gazelle-like, at the same speed as her mum's car, Janey rushed past familiar landmarks until, in the wink of an eye, she found herself approaching the school gates. To slow herself down she grabbed at a railing, and then at another.

But the Fleet-feet didn't stop. Instead Janey ploughed through the gates, sprinting along at high speed. Fortunately the last children were already filtering back into the school building and didn't notice her. Swerving hard, trying all the time to stop herself by digging her heels in and grabbing at bushes, Janey stumbled to the right and took off along the edge of the school grounds.

Within a few moments she was belting through the little copse of trees in the furthest corner of the school grounds. Janey had the feeling her feet were controlling her rather than the other way round. Any minute now she'd be driven at full tilt into a tree trunk. Heart pounding, Janey realized that if she was squashed flat against some huge oak, like a bug on a windscreen, she probably wouldn't even be found for days. Veering round tree trunks as best she could, Janey saw that the trees were getting closer and closer together.

Then, with a shout of relief, Janey suddenly remembered what G-Mamma had said. On the next step she launched herself as high as possible into the air and, bringing both feet together, she drove them as hard as she could down on to the ground. There was a small thud like an exploding firework and Janey found herself sailing up through the air, straight into a tangle of branches overhead. She clung on miserably, looking down at the distant ground.

'Help! Somebody help me!' she cried pitifully. 'I'm stuck!'

There were so many twigs and branches sticking into her that she felt like a voodoo doll and, below, the long, long drop to the ground loomed endlessly. Just then, to Janey's complete amazement, someone did appear: Freddie Lear. Again. Where on earth did he come from? thought Janey.

'Thanks,' she said breathlessly, as Freddie helped her down.

Freddie looked at the smooth trunk of the tree, and then at the smooth soles of Janey's shoes. 'How did you get up there?'

'Climbed up one tree, then jumped across and couldn't get down.' Janey didn't know if this sounded plausible, but as there was no other explanation she hoped that he'd swallow it.

Freddie looked down his small nose at her. 'Good job I was nearby.'

'Yeah,' said Janey. 'Why aren't you in school?'

'I like it out here. And anyway, I don't need school,' he answered as fiercely as he could in his light voice. 'I'm clever enough already.'

There was no answer to that. 'Hey, I think your sister was just having tea with my mum. Maybe they're going to be friends.'

Freddie grunted. 'How would I know? I'll give you some advice though, Janey, seeing as we're getting so pally. I wouldn't do any more tree-climbing, if you can't even get down. I won't always be around to help out, you know.'

And with that Freddie pulled a nail file from his pocket and sawed at a snagged fingernail as he walked away. Janey grinned and ran back to school.

By the time she finally reached the classroom, Janey was late. She was already stammering her apologies as she tumbled through the door.

'Sorry, miss. I . . . I tried climbing a tree and I got stuck.'

The whole class shouted with laughter, pointing past her at the teacher. Janey turned to look at Miss Rale, only to find an amused male teacher staring at her in mock disgust.

'Well, I don't have a problem with tree-climbing. I was a kid once, you know. But I do object to being called "miss"!'

The class erupted again. Janey felt as though her regular nightmare was just about to happen for real: any minute now she'd look down to find she was wearing her pink tutu and she'd hear a piano limbering up for the national anthem. 'I'm sorry, um, sir. I thought you were Miss . . . I mean, Miss Rale usually . . . I'm sorry.'

The teacher took pity on her. 'Miss Rale should be back in a day or two. Take your seat, please. And you lot, stop laughing. Let's turn to page thirty-two, shall we?'

9 the slippery slope

As she walked out of the school gates that afternoon Janey was stopped in her tracks by a large hand on her shoulder. It was the headmistress. 'Janey Brown, isn't it?'

Janey looked round, wide-eyed. 'Yes, Mrs Halliday.'

The headmistress smiled kindly, but Janey was horrified to see that, close up, her teeth were as sharp as knitting needles, gurning down at her like a craggy mountain range. Other than that, Mrs Halliday was like an older, female version of Alfie – tall, athletic, with thick chestnut hair and eyes like a spaniel. Janey hoped Alfie was going to take better care of his teeth than his mother evidently had. 'I've just been checking up on a few things, Janey, and realized that you are new to Winton, just like Alfie and me. How are you settling in?'

'Oh. Fine.' Janey hoped that saying as little as possible would help her to avoid saying the wrong thing.

Mrs Halliday put her hand back on Janey's shoulder. 'Oh, good. I was a little worried: Alfie seems to think you spend a lot of time on your own. Anyway, we "newies" need to stick together, don't you think? Perhaps you and

your mother would like to join us for tea sometime?
Tomorrow, perhaps?'

Janey couldn't think of anything worse, but it seemed
unwise to refuse the headmistress. 'Oh. Thank you. I'll ask
my mum.'

Beaming her scary smile, Mrs Halliday nodded.
'Marvellous! Just let Alfie know if there's a problem.'

Janey nodded with a nervous grin and then ran out of
the grounds. To her great relief her mother was leaning
against her cheerful yellow car, waiting for her. Seeing
Janey's expression, she frowned. 'What on earth is wrong?
You look like you're going to be sick!'

'We've been invited to tea with the headmistress.'

Her mother was amazed. 'What? Is that usual?'

'No, I don't think so. It's because I . . . we're new to
the area. Like they are.'

'Oh!' replied Mrs Brown, strapping herself into the
car and starting the engine. 'How nice of them! Maybe
you could make friends with the son – Alfie, isn't it?'

'I don't want to! I don't want to be his friend!' yelled
Janey, staring with wild eyes across the car from the
passenger seat.

Her mother stared back, stunned at Janey's outburst.
'All right, all right! You can choose your own friends,
of course. Just thought he looked like a nice boy, that's
all.'

Janey suspected he was more like the kind of boy
who would put dead flies in scones instead of raisins,
but she kept the thought to herself.

79

Once at home, Janey considered knocking on G-Mamma's door, but thought better of it when she saw how her mother scowled across the fence at their new neighbour's house. Instead she dropped her school bag in the hall, planning to go through the fireplace. 'Just going upstairs, Mum,' she shouted.

Glad that the Fleet-feet had stopped slamming her straight into large, stationary objects, Janey bounded up the stairs two at a time. But just as she reached the top, disaster struck. The grip on the Fleet-feet seemed to have disappeared completely, leaving the soles of Janey's shoes like newly polished mirrors. As her right foot stretched out to connect with the carpet on the landing, her toes slid away from her, and shot so high into the air she almost kicked the lampshade. Wheeling over her head, Janey's leg drove her body round in a clumsy somersault, and with a wallop she crunched on to the back of her neck and tumbled, curled like a hedgehog, all the way back down to the bottom of the stairs. She lay there in a bundle, too stunned even to cry.

'Oh my life! Janey! What happened? Are you OK? Oh, say something, say something! Please don't have broken your neck! Please don't!' Her mother fell to her knees, slapping Janey's cheeks and waggling her head to and fro as she watched for signs of concussion in her daughter's eyes.

'Mum,' croaked Janey, starting to cough. 'Mum, stop it! I'm OK, I think. Anyway, I don't think you're meant to shake people's heads if they've broken their necks.'

'Oh, of course not! What am I doing? Sorry, darling, I just panicked when I heard all that crashing.'

Janey checked her body mentally. Everything hurt, but nothing felt broken. Wincing, she pushed off her shoes.

'It was probably those old school shoes,' said her mother. 'They're so worn, the soles must be useless. I'll get you a new pair soon. Miss Lear offered me some more cleaning at St Earl's school today, so I should be able to afford it before too long. Let's have a look at the culprits, shall we?'

Mrs Brown grabbed at Janey's feet. Janey tried to pull them away, but her mother's grip was surprisingly steely. As her mum turned the shoes over, Janey held her breath and closed her eyes. What if the Fleet-feet pads came off in her mum's hands?

There was only silence. Janey opened one eye and looked down at her shoes, and was amazed to see that now they looked just like her normal, scuffed, dull-soled school sandals. She clambered to her feet and went carefully up the stairs before her mother could stop her. Sure enough, the Fleet-feet pads were lying side-by-side on the landing. Quickly picking them up and stuffing them in her pocket, Janey glanced round at her mum and noticed something else. But Mrs Brown had followed, and got to it first.

'Oh, Janey! A wet bar of soap! I must have dropped it when I was doing the bathroom earlier. I'm so sorry! I nearly killed you. Imagine that, killing your own daughter with cleanliness!'

'Don't be silly, Mum. I'm all right.'

And she was. Janey hadn't even felt that familiar burning-nose sensation that told her tears were on the way. Right now, she just felt angry. How had G-Mamma managed to supply her with gadgets that had put her, twice in one day, into mortal danger?

'I'll put the kettle on,' said Mrs Brown. 'Make you some hot, sweet tea. Sugar's good for shock. If that whacko next door hasn't taken it all, of course.'

'I'd rather just go and have a sleep, Mum,' said Janey.

'Sleep?' shrieked her mum. 'You must be concussed!'

'No, I'm OK. Just a bit shaken. I'll come down later though.'

It took a few minutes to convince her mum that it really was all right for her to go and have a quick nap. As soon as she reached her bedroom, Janey stepped up to the fireplace, tapped sharply on the patch of wall – which she'd identified as being at two o'clock from the right-hand edge of the mantelpiece – and wriggled through the tunnel into G-Mamma's. From her position at her make-up bench, G-Mamma looked at her with an air of surprised amusement.

'So, Blonde-girl,' beamed G-Mamma, stroking shocking-pink eye-dazzle on to her right eyelid, 'managed to track down Solomon?'

Janey paused, then spoke slowly, ignoring G-Mamma's question. 'G-Mamma, why, if you are who and what you say you are, would you try to KILL ME?'

G-Mamma toppled from her tall stool and stumbled

against the central lab bench. 'Kill you? KILL YOU? Blonde, I am here to *save* your sorry behind, not kill you! What are you talking about?' Her chins were wobbling furiously, and Janey realized with a shock that G-Mamma might be about to cry.

'The Fleet-feet — I borrowed them earlier. First they tried to run me into a tree, and then they threw me from the landing all the way down the stairs. I could have broken my neck. Twice!'

G-Mamma rolled her eyes. 'Oh, the Fleet-feet! They were faulty, Janey. Faulty. I'd left them out to get them repaired or replaced. I'm always breaking the SPI-buys. Gets me into terrible diddly doo-doo. And they did it twice?'

Janey nodded and threw the Fleet-feet pads on to the bench.

'I'm a super-sized Solomon sausage. I shouldn't have left them out. Sorry, Blonde-girl.' G-Mamma pulled a soppy face.

Janey paused. 'Well, I suppose I shouldn't just have taken them without you being here. I'm sorry too. Anyway, I'm sure I'll feel better after a Wower.'

'So, did you find out anything new while you were spuddling around in the trees?' asked G-Mamma hopefully.

'Well, you were right about those presents from Uncle Sol being SPI-buys.' Janey explained how she had discovered the invisible ink and the message her uncle had scrawled on the frog picture.

'I know it doesn't look like much, Janey,' said

G-Mamma, 'but there's got to be more to this scribble than meets the eye. Solomon would never need to tell his secretary what to do. What could it really mean?'

Janey shrugged. 'I'm still thinking . . .'

'Hmm.' G-Mamma tapped her teeth.

'Maybe . . . Aaargh—' Janey's thoughts were suddenly interrupted as a wild furred beast leaped up on to the counter, glowering at her with hypnotic green eyes and flashing a fine set of fangs. Instinctively, Janey shoved G-Mamma behind her and stretched out her arms to protect herself and her SPI:KE.

'Get back!' she managed to hiss.

The feline face – some kind of chubby little lynx or mini-mountain lion – stared back at her. Then a pink tongue darted from between its lips and licked the end of its nose anxiously. It was actually quite cute.

'At ease, Blonde. It's just the kitty.'

Janey shook her head. 'He looks so much bigger now. His legs are thicker than mine!'

'Well, there's only one cat round here. Your uncle's. His name is Trouble.'

Trouble began casually cleaning behind his ears, apparently unaware that the attention was on him.

'He's definitely a very unusual cat,' said G-Mamma, tickling him under the chin. 'Hates mice, loves water. Don't you, Twubbly-wubbly?'

Janey smiled. G-Mamma and Trouble were practically rubbing noses, cooing ecstatically at each other. Janey had always wanted a pet, but her mum said it wouldn't be fair as they were both out all day. Which reminded her – her mum would be wondering where she was. But she and G-Mamma had work to do. The writing on the frog picture was their only lead and they had to make some sense of it. So, with Trouble between them, Janey and G-Mamma sat at the bench and thought. And thought. Janey repeated what she had read over and over again. 'Hi Brenda, cld you put this in ENVELOPE & send to Janey? Thx, Sol.'

Seconds later, the grey mist shrouding her brain cleared. 'ENVELOPE!' she yelled. 'With a capital E-N-V-E-L-O-P-E. I think it's the envelope that's important!'

'What?' G-Mamma looked on in bewilderment as Janey threw herself back through the fireplace and headed for her bed. Moments later she reappeared, clutching the gooey envelope in which the frog picture had been sent.

'I hid it under my mattress before my mum could chuck it out. I thought it was just the picture that mattered – and I still think the frog has to mean *something* – but maybe the envelope is what the message is about.'

'Whoo!' yelled G-Mamma. Trouble miaowed loudly. 'You could be on to it, Blonde-girl! But did you blow your nose on it or something? Why's it all slimy?'

Janey pulled a face, turning the envelope over and over in her hands as she looked for clues. The pale slime appeared to be turning purple. 'It came out of the school bin like that. There's all sorts of disgusting gloopy stuff in there.'

'Well, never mind that,' said G-Mamma, hopping

around and making the floorboards creak alarmingly. 'What does it say?'

But they could see nothing. They drenched it in invisible-ink antidote, but there were no new hidden messages. Scanning it through G-Mamma's computer system told them nothing either.

'I don't know, G-Mamma,' said Janey, bitterly disappointed. 'Maybe it is just a plain old envelope. A boring envelope with a scribbled address. Some stamps. It's rubbish.'

But as she spoke, an image sprang into her mind like a movie scene and the very words she had said to the postman sprang to her lips: 'I haven't got a five-pence piece, but I can give you ten.'

'I beg your pardon?' said G-Mamma.

Hands shaking slightly, Janey turned the envelope over. The Queen's face stared back at her, sombre and proud. 'This is it! The stamps. There's writing between the stamps! A number four and two quarter signs. I noticed it before and I thought it meant I owed the postman more money, but it doesn't. It's a message from Uncle Sol!'

'But what in the name of Blonde does it say?' G-Mamma snatched the envelope, scanning it furiously. 'Oh, silly Sol! I know we're all SPIs, but sometimes his clues are too cryptic even for me!'

'But not for me.' Janey felt like whooping with delight as she grabbed the envelope back. 'I knew it! He's trained me, G-Mamma. Years ago he sent me a book of puzzles and dingbats, to get me started. And I've been hooked on them ever since. Now I have to work it out. Don't you see? It's a dingbat!'

G-Mamma raised an eyebrow. 'I think maybe you're the dingbat.'

'No, I'm not – I'm brilliant! I've got it! G-Mamma, I have got it!'

Janey pointed to the stamps. 'Two stamps with numbers between them. What are the stamps?'

'Sticky?' suggested G-Mamma. 'Square?'

'The Queen's head. Each one is the Queen's head. Then there are the scribbled numbers. Queen's head – four – Queen's head – two quarters. Head – four – head – quarters.'

G-Mamma went green. 'Oh my life, he's telling us they're going to kill him! Hung, drawn and quartered – is that what it means?'

'No, birdbrain!' Janey shook the envelope, delighted. 'You don't get it! He's telling me what to do. Head for headquarters. And the Sol's Lols logo is printed right here. Look, Uncle Sol's smiley face! He must mean the Sol's Lols headquarters!'

'Blonde!' yelled G-Mamma, almost swooning with excitement. 'You are so right! You've got it! Head for Sol's Lols headquarters! But when?'

'I don't know,' said Janey, a little deflated.

'Right. Let me see that.' G-Mamma wrenched the envelope from Janey, and nodded. 'Birdbrain, huh? Look at the postmark.'

'The postmark?'

G-Mamma nodded smugly. 'It's a false postmark. Look, normally the date and time would be when the letter is sorted at the post office. Well, that must have been over a week ago. And this is dated later than that. Look, 23/4, 11 p.m. No one would send a letter at 11 p.m. That must be when you're meant to be there.'

'But . . . isn't tomorrow the twenty-third?' gulped Janey.

'Yes! Yeehah!' G-Mamma leaped to her feet.

'We worked it out, uh huh, uh huh,
There is no doubt, uh huh, uh huh.
And so tomorrow, Blonde-girl, Blonde-girl,
You're on your way, uh huh, uh huh!'

After G-Mamma had given her a high-five that nearly knocked Janey over, they arranged to meet tomorrow to go over their plan for the trip to Sol's Lols HQ. Back in her room, Janey lay on the bed and swelled with pride and excitement. She and her SPI:KE had deciphered part of Uncle Solomon's message – and tomorrow she was going to meet him for the first time. Would she work out what the frog picture meant before she saw him? Would he send her on another mission? Would he want her to do something dangerous? There was just one thing Janey was sure of: her dad's brother trusted her. And she wasn't going to let him down.

satispying

To Janey's great relief, the next day at school passed without event. Tonight's mission to Sol's Lols HQ was weighing heavily on her mind and she kept imagining the moment she would meet her chubby-cheeked, smiley uncle. As soon as she got home Janey threw herself on the sofa and tried to relax before she had to start her homework. She might be a Spylet, but that didn't mean her maths project wasn't due on Monday.

A couple of hours later, as she sat puzzling over her books at the kitchen table, her mother called to her from the next room, where she was watching TV.

'Janey, look. It's that hunky vet, and he's looking at animals that can survive extreme conditions.'

'I'm doing my homework, Mum. I'll come and watch it in a minute.'

'I think you should look now if you want to know what Uncle Solomon sent you. Isn't that your funny frog?'

Janey raced into the sitting room. Sure enough, the TV presenter was holding a frog in his hand that was identical to the one in the picture Uncle Solomon had sent her. According to the vet, it was a North American wood frog.

'This is an amazing little creature,' he said. 'It may look dull, brown and boring . . .'

'Just like me!' thought Janey.

'. . . but in reality it's anything but. You'd never think it, but let me tell you that this little frog is as heavy as a brass paperweight.

'And that's because it's frozen solid.

'And, incredibly, it's still alive.

'Awesome!'

'Well, glory be!' G-Mamma tightened her satin dressing gown and moved closer to the computer screen. 'Isn't nature incredible? It says here that the little frog survives the winter by going into such deep hibernation that its breathing and heartbeat stop, and almost two-thirds of its body is crystallized into ice! It turns into a Popsicle!'

Janey hopped from one foot to the other. With no slippers on she was cold already, and the mention of ice had sent a chill right up her spine. 'I know it's meant to be a cover, but do you think Sol's Lols might be selling frog lollies or something?'

'Euw! I wouldn't have thought so, Blondey. And why the Sinerlesse Group would want *that* particular secret, I'm not sure.'

'Well, it must mean something! Otherwise, why send it? He could have just sent the envelope.'

Drumming her fingers on the worktop, G-Mamma

screwed up her face in deep thought. Either that or she had wind, thought Janey.

'It's a good point, girly-girl. Why *would* he send you this? Something to do with frogs . . . well, amphibious vehicles are pretty old hat these days, and we could get you to breathe under water easily enough. So there's nothing new there. I guess you're going to have to ask him yourself tonight.'

Janey nodded. 'Mum thinks I'm all tucked up in bed, so I'm ready to go.'

'Well, no time like the present! But you can't go on your first mission as Janey Brown now, can you? Out of your fluffy little jim-jams . . . and into the Wower with you!'

Inside the cubicle, glitter spiralled around her, the robotic fingers twirled in her hair and soothing balm tickled her battered skin. She felt the SPI-suit mould to her skin and stepped out of the Wower with a flutter of excitement and another, more unusual, feeling. Was it . . . power? She wasn't sure, but as Janey closed the Wower door she definitely felt a nugget of some new emotion sitting deep in her chest. It was the size of a walnut, warm and electrified. She caught a glimpse of herself in the mirror and smiled.

'I really am Jane Blonde,' she said quietly.

She turned to the pile of stuff that was appearing on the countertop as G-Mamma shimmied from cupboard to cupboard and screen to screen.

'What's all this lot?' Janey asked.

G-Mamma ticked off each item. 'Well look, I know he's asked you to meet him, but someone else might turn up too. You never know. It's not like HQ is the most secret of locations, so better be safe than very, very sorry.' She drew a glittering blue fingernail across her throat in a menacing gesture. 'You're going to have to be well prepared. First of all, I'm setting up the Satispy to get you up to Sol's Lols in bonny Scotland. It's still a teensy bit experimental, but I know Sol would approve if it enables you to make your appointment in time. At least I hope he would! . . . There we go. The footprint should take you near enough to the edge of the grounds.'

Janey tried to see what her SPI:KE was peering at on the computer, but the view was blocked by rippling flesh, set a-quiver by the frenzied tapping of G-Mamma's fingers on the keyboard.

'Hmm. What's that? Oh yes, I see. There's a moat. In case the Satispy doesn't get you close enough or I've got the footprint wrong, you'd better take a Back-boat. Just goes on your back like a rucksack and inflates when it hits water. Don't worry, it's got a motor so you won't have to do any rowing.' As she spoke she strapped the pack on to Janey's shoulders. It was almost weightless.

G-Mamma then dangled a white leather glove in front of Janey's eyes. 'Girl-gauntlet — fabby SPI-buy, this one, Blonde. Now, remember this: pen in the index finger; camera in the middle finger; laser in the ring finger; stun-gas in the little finger.'

Janey nodded, wriggling the Girl-gauntlet over her

fingers as she pointed towards the remaining items on the pile. 'What about those?'

'Hat. Scarf. Handkerchief. It gets mighty-bitey cold in Scotland.' And she rammed the woolly hat over Janey's platinum ponytail before hustling her down the spiral staircase and out of the back door.

Looking out into the shadowy garden, Janey's stomach cramped with fear. 'What's a Satispy anyway? And what's the footprint? How am I going to get to Scotland and back in time for school?'

'The Satispy is super-speedy, I promise you. Marvellous things, satellites. How else do you think you get all your TV pictures so quickly? And news from the moon and all that stuff? The Satispy just zaps you up into space and splats you back down again in the grounds of Sol's Lols, right at the edge of the footprint – which is basically your landing point. I enter the coordinates for the footprint from here.'

'So you're going to send me up to a satellite and put me back down again somewhere else!' squeaked Janey, realization seeping coldly into her brain. 'You can't mean it! That's insane! It will . . . I'm just not ready for this!'

G-Mamma reached grimly for the object in her dressing-gown pocket – a remote control. 'No one ever feels ready for this, Blonde. But think about it – do you feel ready to lose your uncle and maybe even your mum? You've got to face up to it: Solomon wouldn't have gone underground if he wasn't hiding something big. Something the Sinerlesse Group can never know. And he wouldn't have sent for you unless he needed you. You have a job to do. Go to it, Jane Blonde.'

For a moment the world stood still. Janey looked longingly across the fence at her own house. G-Mamma was right. She couldn't stand by and let the Sinerlesse Group get hold of Uncle Sol's secret. Whatever it was. And Uncle Solomon had trusted her to help him. He needed Jane Blonde. Feeling a little current of strength run through her, Janey nodded to G-Mamma and braced herself for what was to come.

Pointing the Satispy's remote control towards the moon, G-Mamma lifted her thumb and pressed down on the large central button. Nothing happened. Almost giggling with light-headed relief, Janey opened her mouth to joke about yet another of G-Mamma's equipment failures. And her jaw fell off.

Janey felt it split away from her cheek with a pins-and-needles sensation, which spread this way and that until her whole body was vibrating. Terror engulfed her, but it was tinged with a strange fascination as her ears floated round in front of her eyes, and her arms separated from her shoulders and drifted down towards her feet. As her body disintegrated, she saw G-Mamma's face, full of sympathy.

'Sorry, babe,' she heard her say. 'It was so much neater with analogue! All these weird digital packets. Good job it's only for secret SPI work. Imagine having to watch your relatives zip home like this after Sunday lunch. Yuck!' And then she was gone.

Janey rocketed skywards in what felt like a mile-long stream of cells. She was sure she was still all linked together somehow, as she could feel the sensation of every toe and finger. Somehow her senses were still working. She could hear the whistle of wind as she sliced, piece-by-piece, through the atmosphere. And she could still see. In fact, with her eyeballs floating separately around her as though she were juggling a couple of boiled eggs, Janey found she could spot stars and meteors hovering above her while at the same time she could look down at the ground she had left behind. Within seconds, gardens were as small as pinpricks, then the whole country was like a jigsaw piece. Then before she could catch her breath there was the Earth, blue, green and white, beneath her.

'Blimey!' she was about to say, when suddenly there was a burst of light from above, so intense that Janey cried out, although her voice could not push its way out of her jiggling body parts. She had reached the Satispy satellite, now looming over her like an enormous wok.

Please don't fry my eyeballs! she thought, as an enormous spasm of energy seared through her.

Instantly, the process went into reverse: eyes streaming, Janey watched in stupefied amazement as her arms snaked back up to hang from her shoulders and her nose fixed itself to her face again. The pressure beneath her feet was incredible, unbearable and seemingly endless. Down, down she hurtled, blue vapour gathering around her as she re-entered the earth's atmosphere.

When Janey suddenly walloped against hard earth with an ankle-cracking smack, she felt like kissing the ground. The whole journey had taken only minutes.

After a quick check that every little part of her was still working, Janey sat back on her heels and looked into the Ultra-gogs. A tiny map had appeared, and on it a red light flashed over the words 'Sol's Lols'.

Breathing as deeply as she dared, Janey took in her surroundings, using the Ultra-gogs' night vision to assess her location. Ahead of her she could see level concrete, which appeared to be a large car park. At the far side of the concreted areas, water glimmered – that had to be the moat that G-Mamma had mentioned. On an island in the middle of the water was a massive building, which appeared to be made entirely of orange glass. The building sat up in the air, wrapped around a huge pole-like structure. Janey spotted the Sol's Lols logo – the smiling face of Uncle Solomon – plastered on to the side of the building.

'It's shaped like a lollipop! The whole building is a great big ice lolly!'

Grinning, she looked around. There was no easy way across the moat. Slipping the rucksack from her shoulders, Janey dipped it into the water. Immediately the Back-boat inflated, turning into a dinghy with a tiny outboard motor. It was astonishingly robust for something that had felt practically weightless on her back.

'All very well telling me there's a motor, G-Mamma,' Janey muttered, 'but how does it work?'

She clambered into the dinghy and looked around. A filament of string lay next to her and, as there seemed to be no other option, Janey seized it and gave it a tug. The motor coughed gently into life and propelled the boat out across the moat, sputtering quietly, so that Janey was able to reach the other side, scramble up on to the bank and repack the Back-boat without attracting attention.

As she neared the lollipop building, Janey used her Ultra-gogs to help her peer inside. Nearly all the offices were in darkness, but she could make out desks, conference tables, computers and flip charts. The stick at the bottom of the building was flooded with light, and she could see a couple of figures inside, dotted around a huge desk. She guessed this was the reception area. It seemed a bit strange that Sol's Lols employees would be at work so late. Looking up, she spied someone in an office right at the top of the building. The light was on.

'Zoom in,' she commanded the Ultra-gogs.

They obeyed, but Janey could make out only a neat pair of hands on a computer keyboard. Could be Uncle Sol, she thought. 'OK, Blonde,' she told herself sternly. 'Get in there.'

Janey Fleet-footed around each side of the building, looking for a fire exit, or an open window to climb through, but as she did so, she discovered something else. On each floor, at the end of every corridor, sat a big shadowy man with arms crossed and feet stretched out. Janey wondered whether these were just night security men who guarded Sol's Lols, or bodyguards

97

that were protecting Uncle Sol now that he was coming into the open. She tutted. Whichever they were, there was no way she could get in through the glass without attracting attention to herself, and she didn't want the security guards to notice her in case they didn't know Uncle Solomon was in the building. Her only option was to obey the first rule of SPI work: do the unexpected. Just as G-Mamma had taught her.

A few moments later, the pair of security guards in the reception area looked up in amazement as a girl walked through the door. She had on a bobble hat, scarf, gloves and rucksack and was dressed from head to foot in a silver snowsuit. Her narrow black glasses steamed up as soon as she entered the building.

'Cold here in Scotland!' she chirped.

As soon as she was able to see through her steamed-up glasses, Janey checked out the two men before her. Both were stocky and broad-shouldered and wore grey boilersuits with maroon badges saying 'S-Security'. Having two of Solomon's own security men in front of her made her feel safer. Even so, she couldn't assume the guards knew all of Uncle Solomon's activities – perhaps they only worked for his ice-lolly company.

As the guards eyed her suspiciously, Janey decided that verbal attack was the best form of defence.

'I'm here to see my uncle. Solomon Brown?' She wiped her glasses, trying to look as goofy and young as possible – like Janey Brown rather than Jane Blonde.

'How did you get here?' growled one of the guards.

'How *do* people get here? Good question!' cried Janey. 'Oh, you know, planes from Heathrow, taxis, usual stuff.' Information popped up into the corner of the Ultragogs as she spoke. 'Well, plane to Edinburgh – had to be looked after by the air hostess, bit embarrassing really. Then I got a train, which broke down.' She raised her eyebrows in a way that she hoped suggested 'Well, what can you expect?' 'And then I managed to find a taxi because the car Uncle Sol had sent for me had gone, obviously, as the train was so late and everything. Anyway, I'm starved! And he promised me a pizza. Can I go up and see him?'

The two guards continued to stare at her as she chuntered on. Eventually one of them picked up the phone and stabbed at one of the numbers. 'Girl here says she's Solomon's niece. He's expecting her, apparently. Mmm. Yes. Yes. Yes, ma'am, I will.'

The guard smiled over the desk at Janey. 'Sorry about that. Gave us a bit of a shock then, wandering in here at midnight. Anyway, I've just spoken to his secretary, and she says Solomon is expecting you, like you said. We're to take you up to his office right away.'

Janey could hardly stop herself from smirking. With apes like these two around, this was all going to be remarkably easy. And with Uncle Solomon out of hiding, the danger must have passed.

lost in a lolly

After her run-in with the Sinerlesse on the rooftop of Uncle James's bank, it felt good to get straight into a lift and just hit a button. Janey could hardly believe that she had rescued her mum just a few short days ago. She knew so much more now that she could hardly keep track of it all.

Flanked by the S-Security guards, she felt very small, but unworried. They seemed amiable enough, chatting easily over her head about what they would be having for breakfast. Janey decided to keep up the chirpy-kid front by joining in with them. 'So, is he nice to work for then, my uncle?'

Immediately the two big heads whipped round and down. The chatting stopped. 'What do you mean?' asked one of them eventually.

Janey cleared her throat. 'Well, you know. He's all jolly looking, isn't he? Looks like he'd be a nice person to have as the boss of Solomon Security.'

As Janey spoke, the eyes of the second man flitted over the badge of his colleague and then back to meet the man's squinting frown. 'Yeah, Solomon Security,' he nodded. 'That's right. We've got a really great boss. The best. Look, here we are.'

The doors slid open. Ahead of her Janey saw a swinging glass door leading to a floodlit room. Uncle Sol's office, she thought excitedly. His chair was facing away from her but Janey could hear the scratch of the computer mouse on the desktop. Janey felt a tingle of anticipation. She was finally going to meet her uncle, Solomon Brown: the great SPI; the incredible scientist; the one person in the whole world who might be able to tell her what her father, Boz 'Brilliance' Brown, had really been like. Her heart thumped heavily beneath her silver SPI-suit.

She was so lost in her own thoughts that she almost didn't hear what the security men were saying.

'Ariel said to bring her into Brown's office, right?'

'Yep, that's the one, mate.'

The words seeped into Janey's brain as she felt a firm grip on her arm. Confusion fell over her like a blanket. 'Ariel? Not . . . Don't you mean—'

'Think I know what I mean, love. I'm not as stupid as I look.' Grinning nastily, the first security guard flung open the glass doors and shoved Janey through. 'Here's the girl. Where do you want her, ma'am?'

Janey felt sick. It was not her uncle sitting in the office, busily working at his computer. This must be Ariel, the power-crazed, faceless leader of the Sinerlesse Group and her uncle's biggest enemy. Beneath the desk squatted a mean-looking dog, a dachshund. It was currently being used as a footrest, and across its back lay a small pair of low-heeled shoes. Had it not been for the way the dog bared its small, needled teeth at Janey, she might have thought it was a stuffed cushion.

'No!' screamed Janey.

She started to struggle. Immediately two sets of vice-like fingers clamped down on her, holding her fast as they all watched the ten neat fingernails tapping away on the keyboard. When the noise stopped, all three of them drew in a breath of anticipation. Suddenly Ariel raised one delicate hand and pointed once, twice, three times over to the right. Then the tapping resumed.

'No! Where's my uncle?' Janey tried to wriggle out of the iron hands of her captors. In the struggle she managed to point her middle finger towards the chair and flick. Without a flash, thankfully, Janey felt the camera whirr against her knuckle as she took a photograph of all she could see of Ariel – her busy, tiny, treacherous hands.

'He's not here, is he? Sorry, you missed him. You were just a little . . . late!' snickered the second security guard. And pinning her arms behind her back, the Sinerlesse henchmen dragged Janey down the dark corridor.

'This is where Ariel wants her, isn't it?' asked one of the guards, opening a door. Janey was catapulted so hard through the opening that she fell, sprawling, on to the cold floor. The door closed behind her and she was plunged into complete darkness.

Her instinct was to cry, but Janey now realized that

the bridge of her Ultra-gogs pressed on precisely the points that she herself would squeeze when she felt tears approaching. Janey could have kicked herself for trying to be so clever. She had walked, like a fool, straight into the arms of the Sinerlesse Group and its dangerous leader. Suddenly the last thing on her mind was crying. Angry that she'd been so naive and so easily fooled by the security guards, Janey felt a cold, vengeful logic flood into her brain.

'Sort it out, Blonde!' she hissed to herself. 'Did you come all this way to be locked up by two oversized meatheads and a . . . teeny-tiny evil woman? No. Did you let your whole body disintegrate and re-form just to be fooled that easily into the most obvious of traps and then GIVE UP? No! And are you going to let Mum discover you're not in bed in the morning and call the police and . . . and blow your first mission entirely? No, no, no!'

Her fury was really bubbling now. She couldn't give up. The Sinerlesse must somehow have intercepted the message on the envelope. They were probably holding Uncle Solomon right now. Jumping to her feet, Janey held her white-gloved hand out in front of her.

'Right. Girl-gauntlet. Index finger – pen.' Janey pointed and flicked her finger, and sure enough a pen nib appeared from the end of the gauntlet finger. 'Middle finger, camera. Already used that. Now, what was the next one? Ring finger – ah!'

From Janey's fourth finger a beam of acid-yellow light arced into the darkness. By scanning around with her finger, she could make out that the surfaces were all shining glass, but the beam was so narrow she found it hard to see anything more. Thinking quickly, Janey directed the finger at herself; light bounced off her reflective SPI-suit, warming her front and creating a glow that reached a few metres ahead of her.

Janey was in a spacious room with an enormous vaulted glass ceiling, which would have let in the starlight if the cloud cover had not been so dense. A walkway of about two metres ran all the way around the perimeter. Luckily, Janey had fallen on to this, rather than beyond it. For the whole of the middle of the room was a vast swimming pool.

Janey lay down on her front and edged towards it. She reached a finger out towards the flat, glistening surface of the water. It didn't move: the swimming pool was frozen into a solid block of ice. Janey took a photograph of the ice, then stood up to think about how to escape.

It was hopeless. The walls and floor blended seamlessly into each other: she couldn't even see where the door had been, let alone open it. The floor was completely smooth, and in the centre was a huge pool of ice, frozen all the way through. She even looked upwards at the vast cathedral ceiling for a possible way out, but it was so high that her Fleet-feet would be useless. Squatting on the floor, Janey looked around, trying to stay calm. It was bitterly cold now and ice had started to form on the lenses of her Ultra-gogs. She looked up to the heavens, but there was no help from there. Only a rocket could blast her through that roof.

'Think, Blonde-girl!' Janey cried. She knew she would work out a solution somehow, if she could just concentrate for long enough. 'Think like a SPI!'

But before her thought processes could click into action, Janey heard a voice. The faintest whisper seemed to be coming from the very walls of the room. It was almost like her own mind was speaking aloud to her, repeating her name over and over. Rigid with fear, she pointed the finger-beam into every corner but could see no one.

'Janey . . . Janey . . .'

There it was again. A low, insistent whisper. It wasn't just in her mind, she was sure of it.

'Who is that? Uncle Solomon, is it you?'

'Janey, get out!' The whisper rippled with the icy tinkle of wind chimes.

'Uncle Sol! Tell me if it's you. I can't see you!' Janey whipped the beam of light back and forth across the room. 'Did my brain cells drop out on the Satispy? I must be going mad!'

Loud voices suddenly interrupted Janey's search. They were coming from the corridor outside. Though she couldn't hear exactly what was being said, Janey guessed that her future was being discussed. Fear rattled up her spine.

'Out. Out. Out.' More insistent now, the whisper echoed around the stark walls.

'OK, but how?' whispered Janey.

105

It was like trying to work out how to get up the side of Uncle James's bank all over again. This time the only equipment she had with her was the Back-boat. There was nothing she could do. Launching herself out on to the ice pool on a dinghy was no protection. Her captors could just skate out on to the ice and grab her.

Then all at once, with a searing flash of inspiration, it came to her. With her left hand she checked the end of her ponytail, then pointed the ring finger of the Girl-gauntlet at the surface of the ice. The needle of light burned into the ice-crystals, and slowly, too slowly, a tiny puddle of water began to form. The footsteps were closer now: Janey could hear them clearly. 'Come on!' she groaned, willing the laser's heat to work more quickly.

But as the door started to open, Janey was ready. Hands appeared around the edge of the door. She ripped off the Back-boat and slammed it down on to the foot-sized puddle of water she had created on the ice. It did the job. Instantly the inflatable boat sprang into being. The security guards heard the whoosh of air and ran into the room just in time to see Janey whip off her hat, angle her head towards the air-filled side of the dinghy and thrust her frozen ponytail into the rubber.

Like an enormous party balloon, the inflatable popped. Janey hung on to the rope strap around the edge as the boat, deflating rapidly and making some very rude noises, shot into the air at immense velocity. It spluttered around the apex of the vaulted ceiling in a few demented circles and, just as Janey thought it was going to drop out of the air on to the shouting security guards, she tugged the string to start the motor. At the burst of life from the engine, the boat crashed through the ceiling and hurtled through the air. Janey could just make out the low, insistent voice again calling out to her . . .

'Destroy the—'

But she had no time now to think about what her uncle might mean. Instead she yelled out into the night sky, 'What have I done? I'm going to die!'

She hung on tight, every sinew in her back straining with the effort. Cold fresh air poured down her throat and she spun like a sycamore leaf, down, down the side of the building, until she landed in the moat with a resounding splash.

Gasping and spluttering, she reached for the surface. The boat had had it, but Jane Blonde was just fine.

'Whoo!' Janey whooped for joy just like G-Mamma would as excitement coursed through her. 'You're alive, Blonde-girl!'

But she wouldn't be for long, if she hung around yelling. From the lolly-shaped building behind her came the pounding of heavy feet. Gulping and coughing, Janey hauled herself up the sheer side of the moat by looping her scarf around the post on the edge and levering her legs up the slimy, moss-coloured stone. Her elation now as deflated as the Back-boat, she dared for just one moment to lean her hands on her knees to try to replace the water in her lungs with air. Then she struck out for the trees on the far shore, planning to hide there until she could use the Satispy to get home.

But two S-Security men were running towards her, out of the trees she'd been heading for. Janey looked back across the moat: men lined the opposite side, and some were running across a bridge that had risen out of the water. Panic rose in her chest. She felt like a diver with the bends. She couldn't think what gadgets she had that could help her now. She was almost ready to turn around with her hands in the air . . .

But suddenly she got a grip on herself. 'No. Come on, Blonde.'

And she took off as fast as her Fleet-feet would carry her, towards the two assailants approaching from the trees.

The men paused for a moment, then carried on running, arms outstretched to grab Janey as she reached them. They were less than twenty metres away. Fifteen. Ten. As soon as Janey could see the triumph written on their faces, she knew she was close enough. In mid-stride, she drew both her feet up to her chest and drove them as hard as she could towards the ground. Feeling the familiar firework explosion beneath her feet, Janey shouted with glee as she sprang up into the air and sailed right over the heads of the security guards in a tight, athletic somersault. She hit the ground again, perfectly upright, and covered the distance to the trees in seconds. By the time the men had recovered themselves, Janey was flying over the perimeter wall.

'Stop her!' shouted a female voice. 'Don't let her escape too!' But the men were too far behind, still thrashing around in the woods.

So it sounded like her uncle *had* got away then. Janey smiled and slowed to a trot as she spoke to her Ultra-gogs. 'Um, Satispy, please.'

A message popped up instantly: *Press remote-control button.*

Janey flicked her hands across her body. Nothing. No remote control, just some woolly clothing and a Lycra SPI-suit.

'There's no remote control. I need the Satispy to work from here. Satispy, please!'

There was a desperate whine in her voice. The same message flickered before her eyes. With a deep sigh, Janey stopped and leaned against a tree. Her SPI:KE hadn't worked out a way for Janey to get home. She was going to be stuck in Scotland. Even worse, she was going to have to call her mum and explain that she wouldn't be home for breakfast, or lunch, or possibly even supper.

Barking instructions at her Ultra-gogs, Janey vowed to give G-Mamma a good kick in the behind – if she ever got home.

'Nearest airport!' Information flashed up on to the miniature screen in front of her. 'Timetables! OK, the last plane is in an hour and a half. Oops, mind that bush. Right, Mum's credit-card details! Online booking! Good job I concentrated in computer class.'

The journey home took much, much longer

than the Satispy trip to Scotland had. Janey was utterly and painfully worn out when at last she got out at the bus stop and sprinted the last few metres home. Even so, her mind raced back and forth over the night's discoveries, struggling to make sense of them.

Janey forced her weary legs on through G-Mamma's garden and skidded to a halt, crashing into the shed behind her own house. Lights flickered on inside the house as Janey struggled to her feet, running into the shadows under the back window like someone from a surprise gardening programme.

The back door opened. 'Janey? Is that you? It's the middle of the night!'

Wishing she'd remembered to do this when the guards had first grabbed her, Janey pointed her little finger into her mother's face and squirted.

'Sorry,' she whispered, dragging her mum inside the house. 'What is happening to me?' she wondered aloud.

Janey could hardly believe that in one night she had sneaked off to Scotland, committed credit-card fraud and then stun-gassed her own mother.

three horrid heads

'Blonde! Get your biddy bottom through here!'

Janey came to with a start. It felt like she'd only just gone to sleep. Blinking blearily, she rolled back the duvet and tottered over to the fireplace. G-Mamma was lying with her head through the partly opened panel.

'You're still in your SPI-suit! What are you thinking? You know the third rule – decode, debrief, de-Wow!'

'Oh yeah!' said Janey. 'But I only got back an hour ago. The Satispy wasn't there to bring me home again, was it?'

'Oops!' Even with her face on the floor, G-Mamma managed to look sorry. 'I—'

'Shh! Mum's coming!'

Janey hastily shoved a cushion over G-Mamma's head and leaped into bed, pulling the duvet up to her chin just as her mother pushed open the door.

'Were you talking to someone?' said Mrs Brown, a hand to her forehead.

'No. Er, singing. To myself!'

Her mother looked at her suspiciously. 'Right. I

was hoping you could nip to the chemist's for me to get some aspirin. I had a terrible night – some weird dream about you being abducted by aliens – and I've woken up with this vicious headache.'

Janey was horrified. She'd never even thought to check if the stun-gas had any after-effects. Her mum's head might have fallen off, for all she knew. 'Course I will, Mum. I'll just get dressed.' She smiled wanly as her mum staggered off back to bed.

A muffled voice hissed from behind the cushion, 'I'll come with you! We can debrief on the way.'

After quickly de-Wowing in G-Mamma's SPI-lab, Janey trotted down with her and out the front door. She hurried along the street, ignoring the glances that G-Mamma's aqua evening gown was getting from the other shoppers.

'So how was Solomon?' asked G-Mamma.

'Didn't see him. But I spoke to him. At least, it felt as though he was talking to me but there was nobody in the room. Maybe he was using a tape recording, or an intercom system. The reason he wasn't there was that he'd had to escape from Ariel, who'd got to HQ before me, and she had her henchmen there and I thought they were Solomon's security guards, and they tried to lock me up in the swimming pool but I got through the ceiling with the Back-boat . . .'

G-Mamma's eyes blinked like a doll's. 'Slow down, Blonde! You're losing me. Ariel was there? So who is he?'

'Ariel's a *she*, not a he. And I didn't see much of her.

Just her hands. She did look quite little though.' Janey passed G-Mamma a carrier bag that contained the Girl-gauntlet. 'I took a photo, I think.'

G-Mamma shook her head. 'This is bad. The Sinerlesse Group must have intercepted Solomon's message, interpreted it and got there before you. I did some checks on the envelope while you were gone. That gunk is lubricant for X-rays and UV scans. Someone had zapped it to see what was inside.'

'It wasn't just gloop from the bins?'

'Nope. I don't know how they got hold of your letter, Blonde. But they did.'

They turned the corner on to the high street and made their way to the chemist's shop.

'Well, Uncle Sol managed to escape. And so did I – no thanks to you and the Satispy. Which reminds me . . .' Janey gave G-Mamma's bottom a gentle kick.

'OK, OK!' For once G-Mamma's cheeks were naturally red. 'I goofed. If I could get down on my knees without ripping my seams, I would. Enough already. Go get poor Mumsy her tablets.'

Janey grinned and purchased some aspirin while G-Mamma visited the photographic counter. As they left the shop, G-Mamma waved a packet triumphantly at Janey.

'Good photo, girly-girl! Look!'

Janey shuddered as she saw once again the small, slender hands pointing towards Janey's prison. 'There's her nasty mutt. And what . . . what's that?'

They both peered at the photo. Running under

the desk, apparently coming out of a drawer, was a narrow tube. It was transparent, only visible at all because of the light glinting off it from the computer screen.

'Hmm, I wonder.' said G-Mamma, pointing a painted nail at the tube.

Janey shrugged. 'I'll tell you what. Uncle Solomon was definitely in the building with me somewhere. I just know it – he spoke to me. And he was trying to tell me something.'

They were nearly back home. 'Like what?' asked G-Mamma, a serious look on her face.

'All I heard was, "Destroy the . . ." I mean, am I supposed to kill Ariel or something? I'm OK with the whole Spylet thing, but I don't want to kill anyone.'

'Don't you worry about that, girly-girl. But this could be crucial. It's another lead, Blonde! We need to regroup, spend the afternoon working on this, work out what it is you're supposed to destroy,' said G-Mamma, striding to her gate.

Janey remembered something and groaned. 'I can't. We've got to go for tea with Alfie and Mrs Halliday.'

'Who?'

'The headmistress and her son. It's going to be a disaster – Alfie thinks I'm completely pathetic, for some reason.'

G-Mamma pulled a face. 'Bad luck. Sounds hideous. Well, you'll have to just keep thinking about what's happened. We'll work on it later. I'm going to do some more research on that frozen froggy.'

A couple of hours later, Janey was waiting for her mum to park the car near the Hallidays' house in the school grounds when she saw a familiar small figure loitering with his hands in his pockets. Freddie Lear walked straight over to her and she glanced round, hoping Alfie wouldn't spot her with Bin Boy again.

'What are you doing here?' she asked.

'Extra bin-work at the weekend. You look awful,' said Freddie. 'Heavy night? Have you started actually sleeping in my bins now?'

Just as she was trying to come up with a clever retort, Janey's eye was drawn to something twinkling around Freddie's neck. It was a shiny silver locket. When he realized what she was looking at, Freddie grabbed the locket and stuffed it inside his jumper.

'Have you started wearing girl's jewellery now?' retorted Janey.

'It's from my parents. They died. It's all I've got, so just shut up,' Freddie said savagely.

Janey bit her lip. 'I'm so sorry. Is that why your sister looks after you?'

'Yep. Anyway,' Freddie continued, changing the subject, 'my sister says that as she's working with your mum, I should be nice to you.'

'Oh,' Janey said. 'And how are you going to be nice to me?'

A little smile appeared at the corner of Freddie's mouth. 'Already have been, haven't I? Who else has helped you out of bins and out of trees?'

Janey had to agree that Freddie always did pop up when she was in trouble. 'Well, thanks. I've got to go. See you around.'

'Yep, you will. Bye.'

A warm glow had appeared in Janey's chest, and she had an urge to leap in the air and shout, 'I've got a friend! I've got a friend!' Instead she just smiled as her mum approached and together they walked up the Hallidays' path.

Mrs Halliday threw open the heavy front door. 'Welcome! Oh, do come in! I'm so glad you could make it! Alfie's been dying to show you round, Janey.'

Alfie, skulking in the shadows along the hallway, looked as though he'd rather be setting fire to his own ears. Nonetheless, he managed a smile at Janey's mum as they were ushered through to the large country-style kitchen at the back of the house.

As the kettle whistled on the stove, Mrs Halliday took a teapot down from the high shelf that ran all around the walls of the kitchen. 'Look! Not a speck of dust. Those school cleaners are excellent,' she said. 'Shame that Alfie's room is such a state they refuse to go in there. Now, who's for tea?'

Janey started to relax. As long as Mrs Halliday's spiky teeth were buried in food she didn't have to look at them, and, chewing cheerfully on her English muffin, the headmistress looked quite ordinary. Janey's mum was settling in too, leaning further back into the curved wooden chair and responding easily to Mrs Halliday's questions with smiles and laughs. Alfie and Janey ate in silence, eyeing each other warily.

As soon as everyone had finished, Mrs Halliday wiped her lips neatly and turned to her son. 'Alfie, why don't you show Janey round the house? It's a really interesting old place. Early Victorian.'

'It's fascinating,' said Alfie, in his usual deadpan voice.

Janey's mum smiled. 'I'm sure Janey would love a little tour, Alfie. Our house is so small you can see into every room from the upstairs landing.'

'Off you go then, you two!' Mrs Halliday poured more tea into Mrs Brown's cup and her own. The children had clearly been dismissed from the room. Alfie trudged into the hallway, and Janey followed with a desperate glance back at her mother.

Rolling his eyes, Alfie stuck out his hand like a tour guide. 'You've just passed through the wonderful, warm, cosy heart of the house, otherwise known as the kitchen. Next –' he flung open a door – 'the dining room. Then the lounge. And finally on this floor we have the morning room. Or as I like to call it, the "get-away-from-my-mother-and-watch-TV" room.'

'Wish we had a room like that!' said Janey brightly. 'Mum and I can only get away from each other in the bathroom. And sometimes even that's difficult!'

'Erm, too much information, Brown?'

'Sorry.' Janey looked around for some

distraction. Fancy talking to the Class Superstar about being on the toilet! Her face flared as she headed towards a small door under the staircase. 'What about this door?'

Janey turned the handle, and Alfie reacted as if he'd been branded with a hot iron. 'No, don't . . .' He clamped his hand over hers and shoved the door closed again. 'Not in there! I mean, it's just a broom cupboard. Nothing interesting in there.'

'Er, OK,' said Janey slowly.

But she knew Alfie was lying. What Janey had spotted while the door was ajar was not a broom cupboard at all, but a set of stainless-steel steps leading down into darkness. What was Alfie so desperate to hide?

'I'll show you my bedroom,' he said quickly.

Reluctantly Janey went up the stairs after him. Maybe if Alfie went to the loo she'd have a chance to find out what was at the bottom of those stairs. Janey looked around his huge room, taking in the piled-up football kit, the wildlife books and the model aeroplanes. Above his desk was a big pinboard. 'Wow, you've got loads of postcards! They're from everywhere.'

'Yep. From my dad. He works all over the world.'

'Do you miss him when he's away?'

'Nope,' said Alfie shortly. 'Look, there's a photo of me and my mum skiing.'

Janey looked at the photograph. Alfie and Mrs Halliday were struggling to stay upright on their skis, hanging on to each other and laughing with their heads thrown back to the azure skies. Peering more closely,

Janey noticed that Mrs Halliday's teeth had been normal when this picture was taken. Alfie picked up a snow-globe paperweight from his desk and stared at it. 'Do you like skiing?'

'Never done it.'

'Oh well,' he said slowly, turning the paperweight over. 'Don't suppose you'd enjoy it much anyway. All that snow. And . . . ice.'

Janey felt the back of her neck tingle. The way Alfie had reacted to the room under the stairs was suspicious. And now Janey couldn't help feeling he knew rather more than she would like him to. There was something about the way he'd said 'ice'. Something about the way he'd looked deeply into her eyes. What if Mrs Halliday and Alfie had separated Janey and her mother on purpose? What if Alfie was up here foraging for information from her, holding a hefty snow-globe in quite a threatening way, and Needle-Teeth was at work on her mum downstairs? 'Stay cool, Blonde,' Janey imagined G-Mamma saying. 'Don't give anything away.'

'Yeah,' she answered as jauntily as she could, 'all that cold stuff. Yuck. Who needs it? Let's go and find out what they're up to downstairs, shall we?' Spinning around, she opened the door smartly and headed down the stairs.

Alfie ran after her across the landing. 'Janey, wait . . .'

But she was already downstairs near the end of the corridor and could see her mother's serious expression as she talked with Mrs Halliday. As

Janey approached, she saw the headmistress's hand reach across the table for a large carving knife. She was picking it up. She was pointing it towards her mother. She was plunging it downwards in a terrifying arc—

'No!' Janey yelled, charging headlong into the kitchen. But as she ran through the doorway, there was a scraping sound above her and suddenly something huge and heavy struck her head with a mighty clamour. Janey fell to her knees, dazed.

'Oh, Janey! How dreadful! How on earth did that happen? I am so, so sorry.' Mrs Halliday stood in horror with her hand over her mouth while Mrs Brown fell to her knees beside Janey.

'Mum, you're waggling my head again . . .'

'I am! Sorry! Are you OK? Oh Janey, you poor sweetheart! Why do these things keep happening to you?'

Janey rubbed her head; a large bump was already apparent under her thin hair and she could feel a warm slick of blood against her fingers. The large metal bucket that had fallen off the shelf and on to her skull lay on its side near the fridge. 'I'm all right, Mum. Honestly. I'm fine.'

Alfie picked up the bucket. 'Wow! That is one heavy bucket! Can't believe you weren't completely knocked out!'

'Alfie!' said Mrs Halliday sharply. 'I don't think that's very helpful, do you? Now, help Janey up and we'll take a look at that cut.'

But Mrs Brown had other ideas. 'Look, I think I'll just

take her round to casualty. You can't be too careful with head injuries, can you? Sorry to have to go so soon!'

'Of course. You must put your mind at rest,' said Mrs Halliday. 'Please give me a call later and let me know how Janey is. I'm so ashamed that something like this should happen here, when we were so keen to help Janey settle in! Here, take that slice of cake I was just about to cut for you.'

Mrs Halliday handed them their coats, along with a napkin-wrapped chunk of carrot cake, and showed them to the door while Alfie studied the bucket. Janey's head throbbed with pain, but still she ran for the car, desperate to get away from the Hallidays' house.

Mrs Brown got into the driver's seat, rubbed Janey's hand anxiously and turned on the ignition. 'Right, hospital for you, young lady.'

'No, I'm fine. I just want to go home.'

But her mother was not to be placated. After about an hour, during which Janey heard the metallic clang of the bucket a thousand times in her head, the doctor finally confirmed that her skull had not been smashed, she didn't have concussion and she should just go home and rest.

Later, her mum pulled the duvet up to Janey's chin and resettled the bag of frozen peas on her swollen head. 'Do you know, Mrs Halliday was just asking me if anything was worrying you, when all that happened. She thought you seemed very tired and a little distracted, and was asking why that might be. You would tell me, wouldn't you, darling, if there was something wrong?'

'Of course I would,' replied Janey weakly. If only I could, she thought.

'It's nothing to do with our new next-door neighbour, is it?'

'No. I'm fine, really. I even made a friend today!'

'Oh, great! I do think Alfie seems a nice young man.'

'Not Alfie! Freddie. You know – Miss Lear's little brother.'

Her mother smiled. 'Well, that's very nice. But I'm sure Alfie would like to be friends too.'

Janey just smiled. She couldn't help thinking that what Alfie would really like was something quite different.

After Mrs Brown had left the room, Janey lay in the dark listening to her thumping head. As soon as she heard her mum's bedroom door click shut, she clambered out of bed and through the tunnel into G-Mamma's. Bump or no bump, she had to let G-Mamma know her suspicions about the Hallidays.

G-Mamma promised to check out the Hallidays' house when they were back at school on Monday, and Janey leaped into the Wower for a soothing few minutes. It stopped the pain in her head, and Janey looked forward to telling her mum that the disappearance of the big bloody lump was all down to her brilliant frozen-pea cure.

13 tea and sympathy

Janey slept for most of Sunday.

'You're ill,' said her mother. 'No school for you to-morrow.'

Janey stopped her face from breaking into a huge smile. A chance to get back to SPI work!

The next morning she lay still, trying to look as peaky as possible, while her mother fussed around her.

'Now, you are to stay in bed. And don't let any strangers in. Or, let me correct that – don't let anyone strange in.' Mrs Brown flicked her head wildly towards G-Mamma's house. 'I'll be back at lunchtime – maybe you could get up then.'

The door slammed as her mum hurried off to work. Seconds later Janey heard the fireplace panel sliding up and G-Mamma's contorted face and fleshy neck appeared like a live gargoyle. 'Sweet Solomon, child. Get your booty over to my side, will you? I just cannot fit through here.' Janey shimmied through the opening.

'I thought you were going to have it made taller?'

'I was.' G-Mamma bit into a large doughnut,

dribbling jam down her chins. 'But your uncle Solomon has to sign off on all SPI-doors, and as we know your uncle Solomon—'

'Is in hiding.' Janey refused the Danish pastry G-Mamma was waving at her and plonked herself down at the counter. She giggled when she realized that the red gloop bubbling away in a glass jar was raspberry jam, with which G-Mamma was steadily refilling her doughnut. 'Do you think he's . . . well, is he still alive?'

'We don't know, Blonde-girl. You're the only one who's heard from him. But the Sinerlesse Group will get hold of him again – and Ariel will be even more cheesed off since she messed up the chance to catch you both in Scotland. We need a new lead for you, B. And I need to get on to those Hallidays sharpish.'

Janey thought seriously. 'I know this is a silly question, but has anyone checked his home?'

'It's not such a silly question.' G-Mamma chewed and waved her hands around, flicking sugar about the room. 'It would be so obvious that nobody would think of it, would they? Problem is, honey-mine, that nobody, but nobody, knows where Uncle Solomon's home is. I've never even met him, let alone found out where he lives.'

'With a face like that, he should live with Santa at the North Pole,' said Janey, thinking of the Sol's Lols logo.

G-Mamma's eyes brightened. 'That's as good a place to start looking as any. Good work, Blonde. Get ready to go tonight. I'll have your equipment ready – I'm sure I've got a tunnelling snowplough around here somewhere . . .'

'I was joking!' Janey's eyes bulged at the thought of a Satispy trip to the North Pole, stopping to ask any of Santa's elves she met if they were her uncle. Thankfully, before G-Mamma could talk her into it, she heard the doorbell ringing back in her own house. 'Better go and see who that is!'

'Be careful!' spluttered G-Mamma through the remains of her doughnut. Janey gave her the thumbs-up and hurried through the fireplace. Putting on her dressing gown, she went downstairs to the front door and peered through the spyhole on tiptoe.

There was nobody there. Then suddenly the doorbell bonged again, right in Janey's ear. She put the safety chain on the door and opened it enough to peer through.

'Didn't see you this morning,' said a husky voice. 'Thought you might have fallen into something again and need my help to get out. You OK?'

'Freddie!' Janey fumbled with the catch and threw open the door. 'Come in! Had a bit of an accident the other night, but I'm all right now. You do always appear when I need you, don't you?!'

Freddie grinned. 'Found these on the doorstep.'

He handed her a small box of expensive chocolates, each individually wrapped in a tiny square of different-coloured gauze. A neat pink card was tied on to the box with purple ribbon. '*Sorry about last night – hope you're feeling better. From A and Mrs H.*'

'What's that about then?' asked Freddie, peering over her shoulder.

Handing him the box after helping herself, Janey told
Freddie an edited version of what had happened at Alfie's.
His cheeks swollen with chocolates, Freddie wandered
around the kitchen, opening cupboards. 'So it fell on your
head, just like that?'

Janey knew she couldn't explain too much – there was
no point getting Freddie involved. She might even put
him in danger. 'Yeah, just like that.'

As Freddie raised his eyebrows, Janey was saved from
any more difficult questions by the doorbell ringing again.
Puzzled, she ran to the door. This time, the person on the
doorstep was tall enough to be seen through the spyhole.
It was Janey's teacher, Miss Rale, her sweet face etched
with concern.

'Hello! Are you all right? It was my first day back and
I thought I'd pop out during morning break to see how
you are. Oh, I'm sorry, you've got company,' said Miss
Rale as she caught sight of Freddie in the kitchen.

'Don't worry, come in!' said Janey, grinning. She led
her teacher through and was rather alarmed to notice
Freddie shooting Miss Rale a look of disgust as they
entered the kitchen. Her teacher blushed. As Freddie
stood up, briskly said goodbye and let himself out, Janey
decided she would have a word with him about being so
rude.

'So you heard about my accident,' said Janey, turning
to Miss Rale.

'Accident? No.' Miss Rale sat down neatly. 'I realized
you weren't there this morning, and you seemed to be

about to tell me something the other day – I was just worried that something might have happened to you.'

'Mrs Halliday didn't tell you?'

'No, I haven't seen Mrs Halliday yet today.' Her fair eyebrows peaked in a pretty frown. 'Are you all right, Janey? I'm sure I'd be able to help you if you just told me what was wrong.'

Janey didn't think she could tell Miss Rale what was going on – for a start she probably wouldn't believe her. But she wanted to.

'Look,' continued Miss Rale, 'let me make us both a nice cup of tea and you can tell me all about it. I'm sure it would make you feel better, Janey.' She bustled over to the sink, popping her bag down next to her, and began to make tea as if she was Janey's own mother.

Janey decided that she could give Miss Rale a version of what happened, sort of in the same way she had with Freddie. Some men had been worrying her mum. Her long-lost godmother had turned up. She'd slipped on some soap and hurt her back and then a bucket had fallen on her head. She hadn't had any friends until now and she couldn't bother her mum about it, as she was already holding down more than one job to try to make ends meet. Yes, it sounded like it could be true. As Miss Rale placed a fragrant and inviting mug of tea in front of her, Janey took a deep breath and smiled.

'Oh, sorry, just a minute, Janey.'

Stepping back over to the sink, Miss Rale took her ringing mobile phone out of her bag and spoke into it quickly. Janey slurped her tea as a distraction. It smelt floral and light, very tasty. It reminded her of something pleasant, but she couldn't quite figure out what it was.

Miss Rale tutted and put her phone away. 'Bad timing, I'm afraid. Got to get back to school. So sorry, Janey. I was really hoping to hear about whatever's been troubling you, see if we can't work it out between us. But hopefully we can find five minutes to talk tomorrow.'

For a brief moment Miss Rale put her hand over Janey's and Janey looked fondly at her teacher's long, slim fingers. She couldn't imagine why Miss Rale, so lovely and so pretty, wasn't married already. But her teacher *was* wearing a ring – not a wedding ring, but a large flat signet ring on her right hand. Carved into the oval disc on the top was the initial 'S'. It looked a little familiar.

'What's the "S" for, miss?' she asked.

Her teacher smiled. 'Well, I know it's not considered good form to tell pupils things like this. But my first name is Susan. Don't tell a soul!' she added in a mock-stern voice. 'Got to dash, Janey!'

Janey waved as Susan Rale raced down the path, turned left and hurried along to the main road. Catching a bus back to school, Janey supposed. She was still standing on the doorstep when a voice called to her from down the road.

'Janey! Inside in your dressing gown!'

Her mother bustled through the gate, scolding her for not being in bed, for being on the doorstep in her dressing gown where anyone could see her and for generally not doing anything she had told her to do that morning.

'And you've had visitors, I see!' she said, taking in the teacups on the kitchen table. 'I nearly asked Miss Lear to come round when I bumped into her a while ago, but I thought you might not be feeling well enough for guests. Obviously I was wrong. Janey, didn't I say not to let anyone in?'

'It was my teacher, Mum. I had to let her in!'

'Oh, really? How lovely of her, Janey,' cooed Mrs Brown, her tone of voice suddenly changing. 'What a nice school Winton is! Not like that strange St Earl's place where I've been cleaning for Miss Lear.'

'What's strange about it?' asked Janey. Talking of strange, she was starting to feel a little peculiar.

'Well, for a start, I haven't seen any pupils yet. In fact, I've been there twice now and never seen a soul, even though it's the middle of the morning.'

'Maybe they're on holiday. It could . . . oh! Mum, hel—'

Mrs Brown spun around. Janey was slumped forward in the chair, her head spinning like a kaleidoscope. Her mum's face swam into view and then whizzed away again, her eyes growing closer together until she looked like a cyclops. She could hear her mother shouting, 'Janey! Janey, what's wrong? Oh my lord, your head's swelling!'

But try as she might, Janey couldn't get any words out. Her throat seemed to be closing up. She was finding it hard to breathe. And as the supply of air to her head shut down, she crashed forward on to the tiles.

129

14 truth hurts

Hearing Mrs Brown's shouting and the chair crashing to the floor, G-Mamma shot through the front door like a charging elephant. 'Don't worry, I'm here!' she yelled, barging Mrs Brown out of the way and appraising Janey's state with wide blue eyes. 'She's having an allergic reaction.'

'Allergic reaction?' bleated Mrs Brown.

'Yes, like eating a peanut.'

'Eating a peanut?'

'Yes. Do you have any adrenalin?'

'Adrenalin?'

'Sweet soul survivors, what has happened to you, Gina? Did they blitz your brain of all common sense as well? Look, lie her down flat, I'll be back in a moment. Call an ambulance.'

Within a minute G-Mamma was back with a small silver syringe kit. She shoved Janey's mum aside and administered a dose of adrenalin. By the time the ambulance arrived a few minutes later, Janey's eyes were open and her head was beginning to clear. While she lay on the floor the paramedics did a variety of tests and then drew Mrs Brown into the hallway. Janey didn't attempt to get up, but watched as G-Mamma shuffled closer to the door to eavesdrop.

'They're asking if you're allergic to anything. Told you so. Are you allergic to anything, by the way? Wheat? Penicillin? Your brain-wiped mother?' G-Mamma looked inquisitively at Janey. Janey shrugged and shook her head, screwing up her face as the horrible sick feeling set in again. 'What were you eating? Choccies? These choccies? You're not allergic to chocolate, are you? No? Phew, relief! Life wouldn't be worth living if you couldn't eat chocolate, girly-girl! Oh, listen, they're saying you'll have to go to hospital for tests, find out what it is you reacted to. I'll check things out round here while you're gone. This is a bit fishy, Blondey. Whoops! Here she comes.'

Dropping one of the chocolates into a mug of lukewarm tea, G-Mamma smiled brightly at Mrs Brown as she came back into the kitchen. She pretended to be enjoying a sip of the tepid brown liquid.

Mrs Brown glared at her. 'Look, thank you for all your help and everything, but I think we can let the professionals take over now.'

'Well, pardon me for saving your daughter's life,' replied G-Mamma frostily. 'I'll be off, Janey. Let me know when you're back.' She stalked past the paramedics and out of the front door with her mug of tea.

An hour later, Janey was lying on a bed in the hospital for the second time that week, feeling like a pin cushion after several blood samples had been taken from her. Her mother sat at her side, clutching her hand and cooing sympathetically.

'I'm sure that's the last of them now, darling.'

The nurse nodded. 'The doctor's given the all-clear, so you can take Janey home whenever you like.'

'Lovely, thank you. Now, sweetie, why don't you tell me what you think it might have been? I won't be angry if you ate or drank something that you shouldn't.'

Janey opened her mouth to protest. 'I never eat or drink anything I shouldn't, Mum. And I always eat what you tell me, even those revolting ketchup sandwiches you think I like but which actually I've hated for years. I'm always good. Apart from once, when I was six, I did steal the Easter eggs you'd bought as presents and ate them all myself.'

Mrs Brown stared at her. 'You . . . you said a dog ran in and took the bag!'

'I lied!' said Janey, puzzled as to why she had suddenly confessed to this now. 'But I threw up so much afterwards that I never ate or drank anything I wasn't supposed to ever again.'

'I see. And you don't like my special sandwiches.' Mrs Brown's telephone manner was starting to creep into her voice. She crossed her legs in a quick, vicious twirl. 'Well, Janey Brown, is there anything else you'd like to tell me?'

Janey sighed. Everyone wanted her to tell them things, and she couldn't. But . . . why not? There was so much she wanted to tell her mother, and suddenly she found she couldn't keep anything from her any longer.

'OK. Listen. You might not want to hear this, but I've been sneaking into G-Mamma's at night through my fireplace and I'm going to become a SPI. Uncle Solomon's real business is called Solomon's Polifical Investigations, and I'm going to work for him but he's gone missing, chased into hiding by—'

'You've been sneaking into G-Mamma's at night?' Her mother was scarlet with rage. 'How dare you, Janey? And how dare that wretched woman entice you into doing such naughty things?'

'Mum, I'm not six any more, you know. They're not naughty things, they're important things. I'm a SPI, and I've got this fantastic silver outfit with all sorts of gadgets, and when I'm in it I feel sensational and—'

'Stop right now!' roared Mrs Brown. She started gathering up Janey's things with stiff, spiky movements. 'Not another word of this . . . this rubbish, this . . . this complete claptrap. I'm taking you home this instant, and after I've called the police about that . . . that monster next door I'm sending you somewhere safe, somewhere sensible, where your head can't be filled with all this fantastical nonsense! Your uncle a spy? He makes ice lollies, Janey. You're being ridiculous! Come on, we're getting a cab. If you've quite finished?' And she clattered off down the tiled corridor with such ferocious speed that Janey had to run to keep up with her.

But now that she'd started talking, Janey found that she hadn't quite finished at all, not by a long way.

'It's really not nonsense, Mum, I can promise you. Uncle Solomon's in danger and I've got to find him so I can help him stop anyone ever uncovering his secret project. He's had to go underground. I have to get to him before the Sinerlesse Group do. The other night I had to go to Scotland to find him.'

'The other night? You went to Scotland during the night?'

Janey nodded cheerfully. 'Only he wasn't there and—'

'Oh. And you flew by yourself to get there and back in a night?'

'Kind of. Well, I went on the Satispy, which is a satellite system you can travel on. Well, not you, because you're not a spy, not any more at least.'

Mrs Brown stopped short at the door of the taxi. 'Please, please stop, Janey. If you go on any more, I'm afraid that someone from the psychiatric unit will hear us and I might never be able to bring you home again.'

'But I was just—'

Her mother held up a hand. 'Listen to me. You're going to have to go to Uncle James's house. He'll look after you. I want you away from that G-Mamma!'

Janey was furious. Her mum couldn't send her off to Uncle James's house – it was miles from G-Mamma. She tried to protest over and over again, words flying from her mouth, but her heart sank when she realized her mum wasn't going to give in. It would be impossible to get to the SPI-lab, or get hold of any of her SPI equipment, and without those she would never be able to discover Uncle Solomon's whereabouts, or what connection he had with freezing frogs. Or what she was supposed to destroy. Nor would she be able to find out why these terrible 'accidents' kept happening to her. There was no point in arguing, however – her mum had MADE UP HER MIND.

Mrs Brown was still talking. 'Don't worry about school. You'll need a few days off after the latest disaster. I'm sure Mrs Halliday will understand. And if you decide you really have to go, Uncle James can arrange for a car to drive you over. He's got enough money, and a chauffeur, now I come to think of it. I'll come over every couple of evenings to keep you company. And when we're sure you've had enough rest we'll think about letting you come home. Once I've had social services remove that maniac from next door.'

'What if Uncle James doesn't want me there?' asked Janey, desperate to stay at home.

Mrs Brown looked bemused. 'What's that got to do with anything? He doesn't have a choice! He's my little brother; he'll do as I ask.'

When they arrived home from the hospital, Mrs Brown reached for the phone immediately, rapping a few comments into it before putting down the receiver and turning to her daughter.

'Right, that's fine. Uncle James will be here in an hour to collect you. Go and get some things together – enough for a few days. We can review the situation at the weekend.'

Janey trudged upstairs to her bedroom. She reached under her bed for her small blue suitcase, but instead her hand fell into something sticky. The substance was thick and dark red, oozing in a glutinous puddle from under her bed. 'Blood!' Janey screeched.

Crawling backwards as fast as she could, away from the slick of gore on her bedroom carpet, she reached up the wall behind her and tapped. Immediately the fireplace panel rose up into the brickwork, and she scrambled into G-Mamma's SPI-lab.

'Blood! Blood!' screamed Janey, as she accidentally stepped on Trouble's tail. The kitten roared with outrage, his fur standing on end.

'Will you calm down? And leave that poor cat alone,' said G-Mamma. 'What have those doctors been doing to you?'

'Well, first of all they took a pile of blood samples, and then they looked down my throat, and then they went away and huddled together at the end of the ward, and then they came back and told my mum that they didn't know what it was but I could probably go home, and then I told Mum all about me becoming a SPI, and about Uncle Solomon, and about you assigning me my mission . . .'

G-Mamma looked at her strangely. 'And what did Gina have to say about all that?'

'Ah, well, she thinks you're a nutter, filling my head with fantastical nonsense, and she's going to get social services to have you locked up because you're a monster, and—'

'All right, Janey, I think I get the picture. Your mother's gone completely ding-dong and you can't seem to stop talking. Do you know why?'

'Let's see . . .' Janey took a deep breath; it seemed her sentences were very long at the moment. It was very bizarre. 'I don't really know why I can't seem to stop talking, although maybe I'm making up for being quiet most of my life, and anyway my tongue seems to be flapping away all on its own, and I want to tell Mum and everyone else everything that's been happening. Some of the doctors thought it might be shock—'

'Shock?' bayed G-Mamma. 'Shock my shimmying hips! You were poisoned, Blonde! Look at this!'

Leading Janey down the bench, G-Mamma showed her a large Petri dish into which she had tipped the mug of tea and chocolate from the Browns' kitchen. It looked unspeakably disgusting, like something Trouble might produce. Janey lifted her eyes to the ticker-tape stream of print lying next to it. Following a long chain of symbols and codes that she couldn't understand came two distinct words. Janey gulped as she read them: 'POISONOUS ELIXIR'.

'Yep. Poisoned. And I think I know what with. Here it comes.' The ticker tape was still pouring out of the computer. G-Mamma studied it for a moment, then held it up triumphantly. 'I knew it! SPIT!'

'I don't want to, it's really bad manners,' said Janey.

'No, no, no. That's what poisoned you – SPIT. And a big dose of it too, which is probably why you fainted.'

Janey was confused. 'Hang on. I've been poisoned by my own spit? That's revolting.'

'It's not spit, Blonde. It's SPIT. SPI-T, or SPI-Truth, to use its full name. Commonly known as SPIT. Once it's been administered, whenever someone asks you a direct question, you feel compelled to give them the truth, the whole truth and nothing but the festering, fiendish truth! Someone poisoned you with some SPIT a couple of hours ago, and it won't wear off until the morning.'

'Well, that's just great, isn't it? Where did it come from?'

'Not sure,' admitted G-Mamma. 'Can't seem to pinpoint the source exactly, but it was obviously something to do with what you ate or drank today. I'm fully analysing the chocolate and the tea right now. Do you have any ideas?'

'Yes! Lots! I think maybe I should start calling myself Jane Blonde all the time—'

G-Mamma held up one of her pudgy hands. 'Nooooo. Not general ideas. Do you have any idea who might have tried to feed you SPIT?'

Miserably Janey shook her head. 'I don't know! My teacher came round and my new friend, Freddie, but dodgy Alfie and Needle-Teeth sent me the chocolates, so I bet it was them! And, like I tried to tell you before, there's something even more frightening going on too,' she whispered. 'There's blood under my bed!'

G-Mamma suddenly flushed dark red. 'Oh. Sorry. I think that's probably jam. I scrambled through to get your suitcase with a doughnut in my mouth, but as the fireplace squashed me around the middle I, er, clamped down on the doughnut. Did a bit of a jam dirty squirty. Sorry. And I still haven't checked out Alfie and Needle-Teeth. But I did get your suitcase and pack it for you.'

Janey turned to see her suitcase standing smartly on its tiny silver legs. She dreaded to think what might be in it. Then a thought ate into her brain. 'Hey, how did you know I was going away?'

'Elementary, Blonde.' G-Mamma picked up the receiver of her phone and pressed a replay button. Her mother's voice rang into the room, explaining to Uncle James in no uncertain terms why he needed to come and collect his niece and have her under his roof for an undetermined period. Her orders were punctuated only by Uncle James's miserable grunts of agreement.

'You bugged our phone.'

G-Mamma rolled her eyes. 'I've had some SPI training myself, you know, Blonde-girl. It's second nature, same as it is to check that a mirror has a proper backing on it by putting your fingernail against it and making sure there's no gap between your nail and its reflection. If there is, it's a two-way mirror and you're in trouble. Or, you know, waiting for your host to eat first. Just wait until you've had the the full SPI:KE treatment. You'll do all those things as fast as blinking.'

Just as Janey was about to reply, her mother's

voice sang out again through G-Mamma's phone. 'What? Say that again, will you? You're breaking up. Five minutes? OK, James, I'll make sure she's ready.'

'I'd better go,' said Janey. 'But now what? I can't just hang around at Uncle James's doing nothing. We have to carry on with the investigation.'

'I'll be in touch. And remember everything I've taught you. Now take your case. Go,' cried G-Mamma, shoving her through the fireplace.

Janey hauled her case into her bedroom, pausing for a few precious moments to open the lid and shove in the shoebox holding Sol's gifts. At least she could think about him, even if she was staying with another uncle. How different they were. Uncle Sol was trying desperately to get to meet her, while Uncle James, she was sure, would be trying just as desperately to pretend she didn't exist.

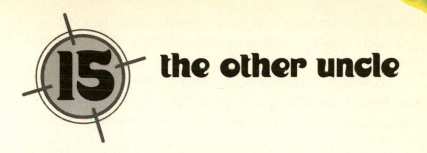

15 the other uncle

Apart from the fact that he looked exactly like her mum but with very little hair, Janey could hardly believe that her mother and Uncle James were related. While her mum raced around doing at least three things at once, Uncle James concentrated on just his crossword, or just his breakfast, or just gazing out of the window at the trees in his garden. Mrs Brown liked to sit and chat with Janey in the evenings, cooking mad things to eat and choosing what they would both like to watch on the television or listen to on the radio; Uncle James liked to go out to the opera or to play bridge at his club with his friend Sinjun (both of which he had to cancel, a little grumpily, now that he was supposed to be looking after Janey). And while Mrs Brown knew quite a bit about children and what they liked, Uncle James knew so little that Janey wondered if he'd ever actually been a child himself. What must his own children think of him? she wondered.

'So,' Uncle James muttered after a long silence in the car, 'what's this trouble you've been having?'

Janey screwed up her face, trying to stop

information leaking out of her willy-nilly. But he had asked her a direct question, and the SPIT was not about to stop working just yet.

'Um, yes. You see, I've discovered that I'm a SPI and Mum and Dad used to be SPIs too. And a SPI is living next door to us and she's training me to be a proper SPI so I can work for my uncle – I mean my *other* uncle, Solomon – who's in terrible danger from an evil espionage group called Sinerlesse and their nasty leader, Ariel . . .'

'Just like your mother,' her uncle commented in his slightly nasal voice, rolling his eyes. 'Typical of the women in our family. Can't seem to keep out of mischief. Although your mum is far more sensible nowadays.'

Janey stared at him, unsure what to say. As he didn't seem to be waiting for an answer, she decided to change tack. Maybe that way she could avoid any further direct questions.

'I'm looking forward to meeting my cousins again, Uncle James.'

'Cousins?' It was if he had to think quite hard to remember his own children. 'Oh, Edie and Fen. Well, they live with their mother on the other side of town now, so you won't be seeing them, I'm afraid. Unless you're still here at the weekend.' Janey gathered from his tone that he hoped most sincerely that she wouldn't be.

As soon as they arrived, Janey was led into the sitting room, where a portly man with a speckled and not terribly healthy complexion was sitting in a leather chair. He was reading the pink part of the newspaper, which Mrs Brown always put straight in the bin or used for potato peelings.

Uncle James smiled weakly at his friend. 'Sinjun, this is my niece, Janey.'

Prising his turgid torso out of the chair, the man delved in his waistcoat pocket and handed Janey a business card before formally shaking her hand. 'Sinjun Tavistock. Pleased to meet you, young lady. Although not so pleased about losing my bridge partner while you're here! Phnuff Phnufff.' He had a laugh like a hippo sneezing. 'Don't suppose you play, do you?'

Janey readied herself. She knew she was still under the influence of the SPIT. 'I quite like playing Twister,' she began. 'And Jenga. I don't play with my dolls any more, but I've kept them all in my blanket box. I play rounders pretty well, though I'm not so good at netball even though I'm tall. I like to play my CDs, but I haven't got a CD player in my room, and Mum doesn't like the things I want to listen to, and . . .'

Both men stared at her, mildly horrified. Uncle James shook his head. 'No, no. I think Sinjun meant, do you play *bridge*, Janey? Just bridge. Didn't your mother say you were quiet?'

Even though she slapped a hand over her mouth (at which the men both looked at each other in consternation), the words forced themselves through Janey's lips and out between her stretched fingers.

'Well, it's true, usually I am pretty quiet. But tonight I've been given some SPIT and if you ask me

143

a direct question I have to answer it. Don't worry, it will have worn off by the morning, or at least that's what my SPI:KE – that's my SPI: Kid Educator – said.'

Uncle James leaned closer to Sinjun. 'Apparently she likes to play "spies". Think it's time for bed, Janey. Off you go!'

Janey looked at Sinjun's card as she climbed the majestic staircase. 'St John Tavistock. Actuary' it read. Sinjun seemed a funny way to say St John. And what did an actuary do? Something dull, thought Janey. He seemed like a suitably stuffy friend for Uncle James.

Janey would be staying in the room that Edie and Fen used when they spent the weekend with their dad. The room was a vast blancmange of pink, lilac and silver, with glitter and girly fripperies littered all over the floor. It even had its own en-suite bathroom – another confection of shimmering pastel, including a gleaming shower curtain embossed with silver and lilac stars. Much further down the landing, Uncle James had his own suite of rooms, consisting of an immense beige bedroom, a caramel-coloured bathroom, a mushroom-painted study and a faun seating area. Janey couldn't help thinking that Uncle James might as well have been painted beige himself, for all the life he had in him.

Still wearing her clothes, Janey got into bed and pulled the duvet up to her chin. As she lay awake through the night her mind played endlessly with bits of information she had collected. She went over and over the words she had heard in the pool room at Sol's Lols HQ but could get no closer to working out what she was supposed to destroy. Nor could she forget the fact that someone had poisoned her – someone in the Sinerlesse Group. Maybe someone close to her . . . When she did eventually sleep, a series of frightening dreams flashed through Janey's brain. After a particularly weird one, in which a bucket-headed monster was chasing her through a dark and eerie school where no one could hear her shouts for help, she woke up to find that it was light.

She wandered downstairs to find Uncle James reading the paper in the breakfast area. Janey sat down self-consciously and looked at the table.

'How are you this morning?' asked her uncle.

'Fine, thank you.' The SPIT had obviously worn off, as Janey was able to lie convincingly. 'You must have been up ages to make all this!'

Janey was amazed. A sumptuous morning feast lay before her: warm croissants and pastries snuggled up to dripping buttery toast; scrambled eggs frothed from under a silver dome; sausages, bacon, black pudding and mushrooms were piled up like a bonfire waiting to be lit; and little boxes of breakfast cereals stood in a neat domino-row to one side.

Uncle James glanced up from his plate. 'The housekeeper does all this. Excellent arrangement – she comes in before sunrise, gets breakfast, does the cleaning, then leaves with the chauffeur when he drives me to work.'

'You don't drive yourself then?'

'No, Janey,' said her uncle sternly. 'I have work to do in the car, and I am not one of these foolish folk who believe it's possible to drive and think and talk into a mobile phone all at the same time. Focus. That's what people lack these days. One task at a time, with maximum concentration.'

'Focus,' repeated Janey, nodding as if she knew what he was talking about.

Uncle James pointed his eggy knife at her. 'I'm willing to bet you were trying to do too many things at once when you fell over, or whatever it is you did. You weren't *focusing*.'

Janey frowned and was just about to launch into a defence of herself when a crash from the kitchen stopped her.

'Don't worry, Mr Bell! Clumsy me. Just nudged that baking tin off the shelf as I put in your casserole for tonight. Oh, hello, love! You must be Mr Bell's niece. Hope you like the extra special breakfast I got together for you!'

A kind round face beamed across the kitchen counter. The woman crossed to the table, tucking her oven gloves into the huge pocket that stretched the width of her maroon tabard-style overall. 'Now, you eat that up, young Janey. Look at you. Not a scrap on you, is there, love? Need to build up your strength.' The sweet lined face, topped with bright ginger hair, crinkled with concern.

What was it G-Mamma had said? Eat what your host eats, or something like that. Scanning her uncle's leftovers quickly, Janey lifted up the silver dome and shovelled egg on to her plate. 'Oh, I'm going to eat lots and lots. Think I need some . . . some protein, make me stronger.'

The housekeeper crowed delightedly. 'That's the way! I can see you're a bright young lady. I expect you're going to be a genius like your uncle here, and my dear departed son. You'll go to one of those super-universities like they did. All tradition and black gowns and punting on the river. Marvellous!'

'Those were the days, Edna,' said Uncle James glumly. 'Formal dinners in the college hall. Foxtrotting under the stars at the summer ball. Nothing like that now, you know.'

Smiling indulgently, the housekeeper spoke to Janey. 'Maybe you can do something about cheering up your uncle while he's looking after you.'

'Edna thinks I work too hard,' said her uncle with a peculiarly soppy grin. He looked at the housekeeper like a puppy waiting for scraps. 'So she spoils me all the time.'

'Well, it's true, Mr Bell. You do work too hard. And there's no one here with a nice meal for you when you get home. Now me, I'm pleased to have someone new to look after, with my own son gone. Anyway, maybe you'd help me out a little, dear? Take care of him a bit for me? It'll be nice for you, Mr Bell, having a youngster around.'

Starting to giggle, Janey pulled a face at her uncle. To her surprise he pulled one back, looking slightly human for the first time since she'd met him.

'Well,' he said, picking up his folded newspaper, 'for once I can assure you that I won't be working too hard today. I promised my sister I'd take the day off to keep an eye on Janey here.'

'Oh, you won't be needing the car then? I'll just let the agency know that Billy will be dropping me off on my own today – don't want them thinking I'm making off with the company's property!' The housekeeper picked up the telephone and punched in a number. 'Oh, hello?' She yelled as if the person on the other end was hard of hearing. 'Miss Lear? It's Edna, dear. Just letting you know, Billy will be dropping me off today. Mr Bell won't need the car – he's taking the day off with his niece. Yes, we're leaving now. Righto!' Edna put down the phone and waved as she shuffled out of the kitchen. 'Bye, Mr Bell! Bye, Janey!' she called.

'Miss Lear?' said Janey incredulously. 'But that's . . .'

'Yes, I know, your mother works for her,' Uncle James said. 'It was Jean that recommended the company. She said that if I wasn't going to let her clean for me herself – which obviously I wouldn't – then the next best thing was someone from St Earl's.'

Janey's eyes sharpened. 'St Earl's?'

'Yes. St Earl's Sanitation and Security Enterprises. Miss Lear's company. Your mum thinks they're really excellent, and I have to say I agree with her. Edna and Billy have been superb from the outset. A real bonus, getting the housekeeper and the driver from the same company. Makes life easy, Janey. Good synergy.' Shaking out his paper, Uncle James lowered his head to read.

'Uncle James,' said Janey slowly, trying to make connections in a brain which still felt a little sluggish.

'Ye-e-e-es?'

'Why would a cleaning company have the same name as a school? Only Miss Lear's brother, Freddie, he's a friend of mine. He goes to a school called St Earl's. And his sister's cleaning company is called St Earl's too. Isn't that a bit weird.'

'Well, I expect what happened was that Miss Lear was the cleaner at her brother's school and took the name on when she set up her company. Things like that matter in competitive tendering, you know. Gives the company a distinctive ring. Might get more business that way. Yes, I expect that's it.' He rattled his newspaper pointedly. 'Now, would you allow me to focus on the news for a few moments? I'll be with you in ten minutes precisely.'

Janey slid off the chair. 'I'll just go and get changed.'

She didn't break into a run until she was out of sight along the hallway, but then she took to her heels as quickly as if she was wearing Fleet-feet, flinging herself up the stairs two at a time. Panting, she closed the bedroom door behind her, then dragged her unopened blue suitcase into the en-suite bathroom and locked that door behind her. Only then did she remove the suitcase key from her pocket and open the lid. To her amazement, as soon as she opened it a chunky missile of fur sprang into her arms, sinking tiny needles of pain into her flesh.

'Ow!' she squealed, wrestling with the soft, wriggling body for a moment until she came face to face with a large squirming tabby kitten. 'Trouble! How did you get in there?'

Trouble wriggled again until Janey put him down and gave his head a scratch. He was really quite cute, she decided, with fine yellowy stripes across his brown fur, and large emerald eyes that stared, unblinking, into hers. As if he knew how lovely he was, Trouble rubbed Janey's hand hard with his head, then stalked off to fish in the toilet with his little lion paws.

'I should send you straight back, Trouble. But it's quite nice having a friend here.'

Grinning, Janey turned her attention back to her suitcase. There were no clothes apart from her Lycra Jane Blonde SPI-suit, a pair of lime-green pyjamas that she had outgrown and an outlandish collection of multicoloured headscarves and immense chunky jewellery in Day-Glo colours. G-Mamma's personal taste had obviously got the better of her. Under the clothes lay a large, white, plastic shower head: a portable Wower! Reaching up over the bath, Janey unscrewed the impressive round brass shower attachment and replaced it with the white one. She knelt down to see what else was in the case. Apart from a supermarket carrier bag containing a month's supply of doughnuts and chocolate bars, and a sheet of paper covered in information about the North American wood frog, there was nothing. Certainly nothing Janey could actually wear.

She sat among the sorry pile of clothing and picked up a disgusting acid-yellow medallion necklace with the ends of her fingers as if it was a dirty sock. 'Oh, G-Mamma!' she grunted in irritation.

'Blonde-girl, you there? Where have you been? I've been waiting ages!'

At the sound of G-Mamma's voice, Janey looked around the room, then giggled to herself. There was no way G-Mamma could be in a room this size without Janey knowing about it.

'Stop sniggering at me, Blonde, this is no time for messing! Man alive, you look even more terrible than usual.'

'Can you see me, G-Mamma?' Janey glanced round again, confused.

'Of course I can! And if you look in your SPIV you'll see me too. The SPIV! The necklace, child!'

Sure enough, as Janey brought the foul chunky jewellery closer to her nose, G-Mamma loomed into view. 'Did I activate this?'

The little image on the yellow disc jiggled animatedly. 'Of course you did! Picked it up and said my name, didn't you? That's how a SPIV works. How else would I be talking to you?'

'What's a SPIV?'

'SPI Visualator, Blonde.'

'Oh. Right. G-Mamma, it's just a suggestion, but I think it might help in future if you tell me how things work. You know, in advance?'

G-Mamma looked sulky. 'I forget how little SPI:KE training you've had, that's all. Now, listen, I have to tell you something.'

'No! Me first!' hissed Janey. 'I've found out something here about St—'

'NO TIME, JANEY!' barked G-Mamma. Janey stopped abruptly. 'I need to talk to you about the SPIT. I've run some more tests and I think I know where it came from. And you're not going to like it, honey-child.'

'Tell me!' Janey could barely contain herself.

G-Mamma's face became very, very serious. 'There's no way to soften the blow, Blonde-girl. I think the person who tried to poison you was . . . your mother.'

Janey stared back at her godmother's face, fury gathering in her chest. 'You're kidding, right?'

'I wouldn't joke about something like that. The tests are conclusive, I'm sorry to say. The SPIT was in the washing-up liquid. Then there was the soap on the landing that sent you flying down the stairs, and the bucket that whacked you on the head. They're all cleaning materials she uses in her job. She could have been brainwashed by the Sinerlesse Group on the bank roof. Janey, I think they might have turned Gina Bellarina against her own daughter!'

Rage exploded like a thunderbolt ripping through Janey's head. 'NO! No, G-Mamma! That's my mum you're talking about. She loves me, she wouldn't ever hurt me. She's sent me to Uncle James's so I can be safe, because she's so worried about me. Stop it! Do you hear me? Stop it now!'

Janey threw the SPIV on the floor. Instantly G-Mamma's tortured round face, mouth open ready to reply, disappeared from the medallion. Janey could not, would not, believe it. G-Mamma had got it completely wrong, and Jane Blonde would have to find out the truth for herself. There was so much still to discover: how the Sinerlesses were getting to her; what her uncle Solomon wanted her to do next to help him; what the Hallidays were hiding under their stairs; why she had a strange feeling about St Earl's Sanitation and Security Enterprises . . .

Suddenly Janey thought of Uncle James, probably sitting downstairs focusing on his watch. He would only come and get her if she didn't get moving. Janey pulled on her too-small pyjama top, shut and locked the case and left the bathroom, turning the key behind her and dropping both keys into her pocket.

As she'd suspected, Uncle James was pacing the hall, sniffing discontentedly. As Janey came down the stairs he looked up, then went completely white with shock.

'Well. Heavens. I was wondering what I should do with you today, but I see there's absolutely no question.'

'Where are we going?' spluttered Janey, alarmed.

Uncle James picked up his mobile phone and dialled rapidly. 'I never saw such an appalling array of bag-lady clothes on a member of my family in all my life. Well, I won't stand for it. I'm getting Billy back with the car and I want you in it. We're going shopping.'

an unexpected invitation

Pleated skirts. Itchy jumpers. Woolly tights with rope patterns on them – Janey hated her new selection of clothes so much that she was almost tempted to stay in her shrunken pyjamas. But Uncle James seemed ridiculously pleased with his choices and, as he was paying for them, she felt it would be rude to complain. Besides, shopping made Uncle James uncharacteristically chatty.

'Did you and Mum ever go shopping together?' she'd asked as they wandered round.

'Heavens, no. Your mother used to be far too stylish for me. And of course I was just the little brother, so she couldn't be seen out in public with me.'

'Mum was stylish?' Janey thought about her mother's sensible wardrobe.

'Oh, yes, my word, yes. Well, until your father died. After that, she didn't care what she looked like.'

Janey gulped. It was an automatic physical reaction whenever anyone mentioned her father. 'Was . . . was my dad stylish then? What was he like?'

Putting down the brown shoes he'd been examining, Uncle James stared thoughtfully into middle distance. 'Do you know, I can't really remember. I'm sure he was a very fine chap. But I truly can't remember.'

Janey trudged along behind her uncle. It seemed like his brain had been zapped just like her mum's. 'Well, do you know anything about Uncle Solomon?'

Her uncle looked much more comfortable with this question. 'Ah, yes. Solomon Brown. The enigmatic but stupendously effective head of Solomon Enterprises. They make Sol's Lols, you know.'

'I know. Anything else?'

'Well, he has other business interests. Not things you'd understand, Janey. Have you heard of business-sponsored schools? There are quite a few around now. Instead of being government funded like most schools are, a business like mine is put in charge to run it like a tactical project. That's what I'm doing for your school. Ooh, look at these gorgeous coats!'

'Your bank runs my school?' Janey was incredulous.

'Well, no, the headteacher runs it, obviously. But we provide the business know-how. What we call management consultancy.'

'And you pay for it?' Janey stared with horror at the slime-green mackintosh Uncle James was eyeing.

'Well, actually, it's your other uncle that does that. Your school is sponsored by Sol's Lols. He's organized it all brilliantly – well, with considerable help from me, of course. He has government

155

back-up, and the very best brain in the country – *moi* – to oversee it.'

As they approached the checkout, Janey's mind was whirling.

'I was supposed to meet him to discuss your school the other day, you know,' blared Uncle James over his shoulder. 'We had an appointment at the bank, but then I won that long weekend in Madeira completely out of the blue. Would have been nice to meet the mystery man.'

Janey was shocked. Her Uncle Solomon was more involved in her life than she'd thought. Perhaps he'd planted someone at school to protect her. She thought of the lovely Miss Rale. Could her teacher be working for Solomon's Polifical Investigations? It seemed a bit mad, but so did everything right now. And what about Uncle James's surprise holiday win? Janey wondered if the Sinerlesse had arranged that, if they had intercepted information about Uncle James's meeting with Solomon, just like they'd found out about Janey's rendezvous at Sol's Lols headquarters. So who was leaking information to the Sinerlesse Group? Could it be the same person who had tipped them off about Solomon's discovery in the first place? Or could it be someone closer to Janey . . . someone who'd given her faulty Fleet-feet. Left her stranded in Scotland with no way home. The same person who was now trying to turn her against her own mother. Janey felt sick. She didn't know whom to believe or trust. She'd just have to go with her own instincts. And somehow she couldn't think badly of G-Mamma.

Janey decided not to push her uncle for any more information right now. When they got back to the car, Billy stowed the shopping bags in the boot before climbing into the driver's seat, the peak of his hat pulled down almost to his nose. The chauffeur was murmuring into his phone as he drove, but Uncle James was too busy staring out of the window to notice that Billy wasn't focusing.

Back at the house, Uncle James switched on the hallway light. Something twinkled on the doormat. Janey watched as her uncle picked up a gilt-edged card and strode over to the telephone. He lifted the receiver and began to dial, speaking to Janey all the while.

'Look, I hope you don't take this the wrong way, Janey, but it does appear to me that you're much better now. Completely fine, in fact. And I really do need to get to the office tomorrow. So I'll just give your mother a—ah, Jean, good evening. It's James.'

Janey could hear her mother on the other end of the line. For once not concentrating solely on his conversation, Uncle James let his eyes drift over the card he was holding.

'No, no, Jean, she's perfectly all right. I've bought her some new clothes. She arrived dressed like a circus act. No, that's why I was calling, to see . . . oh, hang on a moment, would you?'

As he held the little card up to the light, his face broke into a surprised smile. He glanced over at Janey.

'Look, I was calling to see . . . if it would be all right with you if Janey comes to a party with me. We've been invited to a ball this evening, it seems. Yes, of course I'll look after her. Good. Janey will call you tomorrow to tell you all about it. Or you never know, they might invite staff too and we'll see you there. Anyway, must go. Time to get ready!'

Uncle James handed the invitation to Janey. A gold rim swirled around the edges of a crisp dove-grey card, with the wording embossed in rich, dark red.

St Earl's Sanitation and Security Enterprises
requests the pleasure of the company this evening of
Miss Janey Brown
(chaperoned by Mr James Bell)
for a celebration ball at Lear Hall, Royal Wessex County.
Start 7.30 p.m. prompt. Dress formal.

Ha! So Uncle James didn't get to go to the ball unless he was taking Janey. She turned the invitation over. In pencil, someone had written her name in distinctive, rounded handwriting that gave her a strange tingle in her stomach. Hadn't she seen that handwriting somewhere before? As she finished studying the card, Janey noticed that Billy was standing there, shrouded in shadow, moonlight glinting off the polished peak of his chauffeur's cap.

'Hope you don't mind a late invitation, Mr Bell,' he said gruffly. 'Edna thought you and the young lady might enjoy an evening out.'

Uncle James beamed. 'Not at all, Billy! We're delighted. Will you be able to drive us over there in a little while, once we're changed?'

'Course, sir. See you and the young lady shortly.'

Janey stepped back into the shelter of the staircase. Something about Billy's voice, and the way he said 'young lady', made the hairs stand up on the back of her neck. It reminded her of someone, but who?

'Well, won't that be a lovely ending to the day?' said Uncle James, interrupting her thoughts. 'Pity we didn't know about it before, isn't it? Could have bought you a dress to wear while we were shopping. See if the girls have something suitable in their wardrobe. Otherwise you may have to go in the kilt and a Fair Isle jumper.'

Janey frowned. And not just at the thought of having to wear one of Fen or Edie's frilly dresses. There was something very peculiar about St Earl's Sanitation and Security Enterprises. How often did small cleaning companies host balls? Janey felt like she was a hair's breadth from discovering something very important. She had to get to that ball, and soon.

'Don't worry about my outfit, Uncle James,' she said. 'I think I've got just the thing.'

'Great!' he answered, running spryly up the stairs. 'Let's meet back here in forty-five minutes. And, Cinderella, you shall go to the ball!'

Janey hurtled into her bedroom. As she opened the door of the en-suite bathroom, Trouble mewed and rubbed against her ankles.

'Oops! I'm sorry I left you for so long,' said Janey. 'You must be starving!'

Showing no signs of hunger, the kitten followed Janey into the bathroom. Remnants of half-munched doughnuts were littered across the tiled floor, which was also dotted with little piles of cat pooh.

'Oh, kitty, that's gross!'

She didn't have much time. Sighing, Janey rummaged in the cupboard under the sink for a cloth and some bleach. 'G-Mamma should be clearing this up. I should tell her you're here. Well, let her do the stewing for once. Trying to tell me my mum's poisoning me.' She cleaned up as best she could. 'No, I can't play now, Trouble. I've got to get ready for a party. Come on, Blonde. Focus!'

Jumping into the bath, she positioned herself in front of the shower head. It was much lower than the one in G-Mamma's Wower, so she had to bend to get her head underneath it, but to her pleasant surprise, it worked brilliantly. At one point it felt almost like the fluffiest of flannels were cleaning and massaging her legs and ankles. She peered down through the glittery water.

'Oh no! Trouble! What are you doing in here?' Laughing, Janey stroked the cat's head as the Wower worked its magic.

There was only one robotic hand to massage her scalp, emerging from the centre of the shower head like an alien's tongue. This meant her hair didn't turn completely platinum blonde, but had strands of Janey's own hair colour mingled in among it. The effect was still tremendous, bringing out the silver-grey of her eyes and highlighting her cheekbones.

When she was done Janey stepped out of the bath and wrapped herself in a huge soft towel. She was still studying herself in the steamy mirror when a throaty yowl rang out from the bath. Janey peered over the edge and clapped a hand to her mouth.

'Oh, Trouble, look at you!'

Trouble was no longer a cute short length of tabby fur. He was long, sleek and handsome. All the yellow hairs in his tabby coat had gathered together so that now he had two fluorescent go-faster stripes running like train-tracks down either side of his rich, chocolate-brown body. The tufty little forelock he had sported on his head had transformed into a full glossy quiff. And his eyes now seemed to take up half his face, pulsating with flashing rings of green and amber.

Most remarkable of all was Trouble's tail, which shimmered with golden brilliance. It looked like the Olympic torch. The transformation didn't seem to concern Trouble one little bit. He gazed at Janey with his luminous jewel eyes, leaped nimbly on to the side of the bath and dropped down into Janey's suitcase.

'Crikey!' cried Janey. 'Loves water, hates mice – that's what G-Mamma said. You've been Wowed. You're my SPI-cat! I love it!'

Shaking with laughter, Janey clambered into her SPI-suit. She looked in the mirror again. 'Hmm, not quite right,' she said. All-in-one Lycra was hardly suitable attire for a ball – and she still had to be recognizable as Janey Brown.

Reaching high above her head, Janey unhooked the shimmering shower curtain and wrapped it around her waist. Stars sparkled against the silver backdrop of her SPI-suit. Then Janey fished among the colourful items that G-Mamma had packed for her. First, she found a long gauze headscarf the colour of lavender. Coiled around her waist, it held the starry curtain in place and made the suit and skirt blend into one shimmering designer dress. Next Janey found a pair of shiny white boots with Fleet-feet soles and a pair of egg-sized clip-on crystal earrings. On her ears they would have made Janey look as if she had mumps, but attached to the top of the white boots they gave the appearance of fairy-tale glass slippers.

Janey picked up the SPIV and put it around her neck. She might be angry at G-Mamma right now, but it was good to know she could communicate with her if she needed to. Against her silver catsuit the SPIV softened from its eye-searing acid yellow to a burnished gold, finishing her outfit perfectly. Even her Ultra-gogs looked stylish. As a final touch, Janey opened the shoebox and took out the rocket-shaped hairslides that Uncle Sol had sent her. She pushed them into her sleek pelt of hair, where they glimmered and gleamed.

'Pretty sensational, Blonde-girl,' she said to herself, admiring her glamorous reflection.

With minutes to spare, Janey reread the sheet of information about the North American wood frog. The creature was truly amazing: after spending two or three months frozen like an ice cube, stopping its heart beating and not even breathing, it simply melted back into life as spring arrived – although they were very fragile while frozen and could quite easily snap or shatter like dropped crystal. What was Uncle Solomon trying to tell her by bringing this incredible creature to her attention?

'I don't know, Trouble. Should I try melting one of Sol's ice lollies? Perhaps . . . perhaps there are more messages on the sticks!' She ruffled the cat's quiff, but his paw quickly smoothed it back into shape. 'I've got to find Uncle Solomon. He needs my help – before Ariel gets to him.'

Shaking her hand away, Trouble headed for the door. On the way, his jaunty saunter knocked over the bottle of cleaning fluid Janey had used to wipe up his mess earlier.

'Trouble! You really are, aren't you? Don't stand in that, it might hurt your paws. Nasty things in cleaning fluids.'

Suddenly Janey gasped. Understanding whooshed through her brain like a firework. She grabbed the SPIV.

'G-Mamma!' she said urgently.

'Checking in, Blonde.' Her godmother's face was blotchy and red from crying, but she tried to smile brightly.

'Let's forget about earlier. Listen, what you said about my mum and the cleaning materials – you were nearly there! I had a feeling before that there was something funny about them, but now I'm convinced. I think it's the cleaning *company* she works for that's dodgy, not my mum. Think about it – St Earl's is everywhere!'

G-Mamma's face loomed large and fleshy. 'Hot diggety dog, Blondette! You could be right! Talk me through it!'

Janey thought rapidly. 'OK. Well, all the things that caused my accidents could have been planted. The washing-up liquid could have been slipped into the house so Mum would use it. And the soap . . . yes! The soap was dropped near my bedroom on the day Miss Lear came to visit Mum. And the bucket . . . the St Earl's cleaners do Mrs Halliday's house! And there's Freddie—'

'Yes!' sputtered G-Mamma excitedly. 'And I checked out the Hallidays too. You'll be staggered! Your little boyfriend and his mum are not who you think they are . . .'

'He's not . . . yuck! Alfie Halliday is not my boyfriend!'

'Whatever!' said G-Mamma urgently. 'Watch out for them – he and his mum will catch up with you very soon—'

'Well, I won't be here!' cried Janey. 'St Earl's is having a ball tonight. Bit of a coincidence, don't you think? I'm going to find out whatever I can!'

'Be careful, Blonde. Check in soon . . .'

Janey released the SPIV and G-Mamma disappeared. As she looked in the mirror one last time, Janey had a sudden recollection of something her SPI:KE had once said. She leaned forward and pulled the mirror away from the wall. It was an ordinary looking glass and while she hadn't really suspected Uncle James, Janey knew that she had to stay on her toes.

After carefully locking her suitcase and the bathroom door again, Janey skewered the keys into her ponytail band and swept out of the room.

# showtime

'Goodness me!' Uncle James exclaimed. 'Is that really you, Janey?'

'It really is!' Janey giggled.

Billy drove them out of town, the broad streets turning into narrow lanes and the dark night closing in.

'Bet you'd like to focus on where we're going, wouldn't you, Uncle James?' Janey said slyly. 'A local map would be good!'

'Yes, Janey, quite true! I always plan my route with the utmost care. I put in pit stops and work in some contingency time, particularly if we're travelling with my daughters . . .'

Not listening one bit, Janey glanced up in the corner of her Ultra-gogs. As she had hoped, a map tracing their route appeared. They were leaving the city far behind. They had apparently covered forty-four miles at an average speed of sixty-two miles per hour. When she realized she was reading about the level of exhaust emissions, Janey decided it was time to stop. Even Uncle James wouldn't find that interesting.

Although he was still droning on. '. . . and then I check the petrol consumption to ensure maximum efficiency for lowest cost. But then I . . . goodness me!'

Just at that moment the car started to slow, pulling up in front of an enormous mansion. Snow was falling. Against a background of white snowflakes on a black velvet sky, the building looked like something from a fairy tale. Immense granite steps led up to gigantic oak doors. You could drive a double-decker bus through there, thought Janey; St Earl's Sanitation and Security Enterprises is doing very well for itself. Linking arms with her uncle, she skipped up the steps and into the Lears' mansion.

'How can a cleaning company afford this?' said Janey.

'Miss Lear must have private means, my dear,' he whispered back, equally impressed by their surroundings. 'I must say, I'm very much looking forward to meeting her.'

The mansion was breathtaking. Crystal dripped from every inch of the lofty ceilings like shimmering stalactites; silver-and-claret balloons jostled along the walls and ceiling, suspended in a delicate hammock over the central dance floor, and all around Janey beautifully dressed people were air-kissing each other and posing for photographs.

A lady with a clear voice that carried far across the decorated expanse of hall was addressing crowds of people, with her back to Janey and her uncle.

'So, just remember the cameras are running at

all times. Just improvise madly, darlings, and act your little socks off like you've all been paid to do. Our directors will give you instructions as we go along. And remember, I'm here for you if you need help.'

The voice sounded familiar to Janey, but she was too busy taking in her glamorous surroundings to take much notice. She recognized a few of the faces in the crowd – actors and presenters from television. That was probably why the voice sounded familiar – it must be someone off a TV show or something.

'We've been personally invited by Miss Lear,' bellowed Uncle James to nobody in particular. A butler in splendid livery took the invitation from Uncle James. He went over to the lady issuing directions and whispered discreetly in her ear.

'That must be Miss Lear,' said Uncle James smugly. The lady had thrown up her hands theatrically.

'Oh, how wonderful that they're here! Janey, can that really be you? You look sensational!'

Janey's smile froze in shock as she saw the woman's face.

'Mwah, mwah,' said Miss Rale, smacking the air next to Janey's cheeks with her rouged lips. 'Oh, don't look so surprised, Janey. Teachers go to parties as well, you know!'

It took a few moments for Janey to recover as Miss Rale looked at them with her usual kind, wide smile.

'Uncle James, this is my . . . erm . . . teacher. Miss,

this is my uncle.' As Janey introduced them, all she could think was that she had taken the day off school and was now here at a party with not a thing wrong with her, in front of her own class teacher.

The two adults shook hands formally and Uncle James blushed as Miss Rale looked him carefully up and down.

'Oh, I can see the family resemblance. So you must be Janey's uncle on . . .'

'Her mother's side,' explained Uncle James, sounding more nasal than ever. 'James. James Bell.'

The teacher nodded. 'He does look like your mum, doesn't he, Janey?'

Janey was confused. 'I thought you'd never met my mum! But, er . . .' she continued, composing herself, 'I suppose, yes, they do look alike. And you look lovely.' Her teacher was as radiant as a damask rosebud in a tight straight dress of burgundy velvet. Miss Rale inclined her head modestly.

'But, miss, what are you doing here?'

'Oh, Janey! I thought better of you. I know children all think that teachers don't have first names, or families, or any kind of life outside of school. But we do! All sorts of different lives. I'm here for the celebrations, as you are. My sister should be here at any moment – she's just been a little held up. Then we can all get going. Will any other members of your family be attending, Janey?' Cocking her head to one side, Miss Rale looked with her usual concern into Janey's face.

And for the first time, this made Janey feel very uncomfortable. 'No, I don't think so,' she said.

Miss Rale tucked her hand into the crook of Uncle James's arm. 'Oh well. Come along, James. Let me introduce you to a few people. And please, do call me Susan.'

'Miss Lear! Jimbo!' called a voice from the dance floor.

'Thank you, Susan. Oh, look – there's Sinjun!' exclaimed Uncle James delightedly, pointing towards his friend, who was wearing a horribly floral bow tie and cummerbund that clashed madly with his violent skin. 'Sinjun!' He turned to Miss Rale and continued, 'It's written St John, you know, Susan, but pronounced *Sinjun*. Strange breed, we British, aren't we?'

'Of course, I know. I wrote all the invitations, and I remember most distinctly writing his name,' cooed Miss Rale, giving Janey a 'run-away-and-play' flick of the fingers. 'Let's go and chat with him, shall we?'

Mystified, Janey watched as Miss Rale led her uncle across the packed floor. She struggled to make sense of what was happening. If it was Miss Rale's writing on the back of the invitation, no wonder Janey had recognized it. She'd seen it on her homework, for sure, but somewhere else too . . . And why on earth had Sinjun called her teacher 'Miss Lear'? She suddenly felt very small and alone, and much too young to be abandoned at a ball. On a spying mission.

'Come on, Blonde, sort yourself out,' she told herself sternly.

On an impulse she backed into a quiet corner and took hold of the SPIV, keeping a careful eye on the people nearby.

'G-Mamma,' she hissed urgently into the medallion. 'Check in, G-Mamma. Look, I can't look down in case anyone sees what I'm doing. But there's something very strange going on here at this ball. My teacher, Miss Rale, she's here. But Uncle James's friend seems to think that she's *Miss Lear*. I don't like it. There's something I'm not quite getting yet. But I will. I'll leave the SPIV activated so you can watch with me – shout a warning if you see anything dangerous. Over.'

Janey glanced around, wishing that G-Mamma would come bumbling towards her in some outrageous rainbow jelly-mould of a ball gown. She patted her ponytail self-consciously and made her way to the sagging buffet tables at the back of the enormous round ballroom.

She had never seen anything like it. Whole roasted animals were dotted along the tables. Salads of every description jockeyed for position next to breads and pies, olives and fruit. Candlesticks as tall as Janey were set out at regular intervals along tables as long as the deck of a ship.

As she watched, the centrepiece was being man-oeuvred into place by a couple of men in white catering coats and hats. One was much shorter than the other and they were obviously bickering. When the smaller one nearly dropped his end, his colleague hissed, 'Pest!' before shoving him out of the way and sliding the whole creation on to the table by himself. Janey could see why he wouldn't want it to be broken. It was magnificent – a gleaming swan the size of a small car, hollowed out to contain sparkler-topped pineapples, and all carved completely from ice. It was lifelike in every detail, apart from the eyes, which had a curious blue tinge to them.

The white-coated catering men hurried away before the party began in earnest. Janey noticed Edna, her uncle James's housekeeper, jiggling merrily in the background, ordering waiters around and lifting yet more food out of enormous wooden crates. She waved, nodding her approval at Janey's appearance, but just as Janey was about to wave back, something made her jump.

'Janey. Trust . . . nobody until . . . I . . . tell you.'

Janey froze and drew in a sharp breath. Although faint and distant, it sounded exactly like the voice she had heard in the ice-pool room at Sol's Lols HQ. She willed her heart to stop pounding so hard, made sure that nobody was watching her, then grabbed the SPIV and peered into it. 'Hello?' she whispered urgently. The tiny screen was blank.

'No . . . not there. Be . . . careful, Janey.' The voice was insistent and, although it was quiet, Janey sensed that it was coming from nearby.

Picking up a handful of olives and dropping one on purpose, Janey bent down and checked under the tablecloths that ran the length of the buffet tables. She could see nothing but table legs and the odd bit of dropped food.

'Uncle Sol?' she whispered. 'Is that you?'

As if from a long way away, the thin voice waxed and waned. 'Yes. I'm . . . here. Take care.'

Janey was stunned, but she had to keep her cool. She wandered over to a side table and studied the seating plan carefully.

'What shall I do, Uncle Sol?'

There was no reply. Drawing further back into the shadows, Janey looked around the ballroom. She couldn't see Uncle James or Miss Rale or Sinjun. She noticed Billy approaching a small huddle of guests who looked a little lost. After a few words from him, they nodded, reached for their champagne glasses and started throwing their heads back with laughter. Acting, Janey thought. Just as Miss Rale had been telling everyone to do when Janey arrived. Perhaps the cleaning company was filming an advert, and somehow she and her uncle and been invited along. But Janey still hadn't seen a single camera.

Just then there was a yap behind her. Janey turned and saw a short, pointed tail wag as Edna leaned forward, holding some food in her chubby, wrinkled fingers. The dog jumped up to reach it, and Janey almost fainted. She would recognize that snarling mutt anywhere – it was Ariel's dachshund. Feeling sick to her stomach, Janey tried to collect her thoughts as she reached for her SPIV. Nothing at the St Earl's ball was as it seemed.

'G-Mamma!' she urged. 'Can you hear me?

I think we've got serious trouble. Solomon is here, but so is Ariel!' She watched the nasty-looking dachshund in its smart grey and maroon coat lunge for Edna's ankles. 'Repeat, Ariel is here!'

real-ization

So who was Ariel?

As Edna fended off the dog Janey scrutinized her hands carefully. Those were definitely not the hands of the woman who'd been sitting in Uncle Solomon's chair. Those had been smaller, neater, sleeker and somehow much more threatening. They may well have belonged to someone like Miss Rale – the woman Sinjun had called Miss Lear. Miss Rale, Miss Lear. Rale, Lear. Could they be the same person?

Janey's breathing quickened. She had never actually seen Miss Lear. She remembered the time when her teacher had come to visit her when she was sick. Her mum had thought she saw Miss Lear in their street, right after Miss Rale had left in a hurry . . .

Backing away from the tables, Janey moved back to the seating plan. She stared at it, pretending to find her place. There was her name, right next to Susan Lear. Uncle James had been placed about as far away as possible.

'Lear,' said Janey aloud. 'Rale.'

Suddenly a cloud lifted in Janey's brain and she gasped. Lear and Rale – they were anagrams of each other. 'Of course!' Janey could have kicked herself for not cracking such a simple code earlier. 'It's an anagram!' Simply jiggling the letters of Lear gave her Rale! And something was dawning on Janey. There was another name that was an anagram of those same four letters.

Earl.

Janey's chest tightened and she clutched the table plan to steady herself. What did this mean? She scanned down to the bottom of the plan.

'St Earl's Sanitation and Security Enterprises,' she mumbled, reading the logo. 'St Earl's Sanitation and Security Enterprises. St Earl's Sanitation and . . . hah! It can't be! It's like a dingbat!' Uncle Sol had trained her from afar, and here she was on the brink of solving the most important dingbat of her life. 'St Earl's – what if you said it like "Sinjun"? Not "St Earl's" but "Sinearls" or "Sinerl"! Yes! Then there's the Sanitation and Security. S and S. Snerl SS. Plus 'E' for Enterprises. It gives you . . . Sinerlesse!' Janey's brain was throbbing and sweat was gathering on her palms.

St Earl's Sanitation and Security Enterprises *was* the Sinerlesse Group! They must have started up the cleaning business as a cover for their secret spy work, just like Uncle Solomon had founded Sol's Lols as a front for Solomon's Polifications Investigations! Janey's brain raced. And if Miss Lear headed up St Earl's, and Miss Lear was Miss Rale, did this mean she headed up

Sinerlesse too? Was the woman Janey had thought was the nicest teacher in the world actually *Ariel*? Janey felt nauseous as realization hit her as if she'd run into a brick wall.

And what about Freddie? Was he really Miss Rale's brother? Could he be involved? Janey had to focus. She thought of the way Freddie always seemed to appear from nowhere. Of how strangely he and Miss Rale had behaved when they had met in her kitchen that day Janey was poisoned by SPIT. She thought of him in his too-short grey and maroon uniform. Grey and maroon. Suddenly those two colours were all Janey could see: the uniforms of the S-Security guards at Sol's Lols in Scotland. Edna's apron. The dress Miss Rale was wearing tonight. The balloons. Her mind raced back to the beginning – hadn't that weird postman been wearing those same colours? Janey had been a fool.

Some SPI you are, Blonde!

She had skipped and sauntered into every single one of the Sinerlesse traps, without a second thought. They'd entered her home as her teacher, as her friend. Freddie had most likely stolen her letter from Solomon that day when she dropped her school bag. They'd closed in on her mother by offering her a job at St Earl's, which probably wasn't even a real school. They'd planted Edna and Billy in Uncle James's house. And their very leader, Ariel, had infiltrated Janey's school. She had a mental image of the day she'd been poisoned. 'Miss Rale washed the cups!' Janey said out loud. They'd been interrupted by her mum returning, but Miss Rale had clearly planned to find out exactly what Janey knew about Solomon's secret.

And so they'd dreamed up a ball, knowing that snobby Uncle James wouldn't be able to resist bringing her. They'd hired actors and filled an enormous stately home with party glitz – all just to get to Janey? They must be getting desperate, Janey thought, to go this far.

But no. It wasn't that. Janey was in a room surrounded by the Sinerlesse Group. She was under threat. But what they were really hoping was that another uncle would come to her rescue. Then they could pounce.

And they were right. She had heard him. Solomon was here, somewhere, somehow.

'Oh, Uncle Sol, I'm sorry!' Janey was horrified.

She'd led him straight into the Sinerlesse Group's lair.

Now she needed help, and fast. 'G-Mamma!' she muttered into the SPIV.

But just then she spotted Billy making his way across the room towards her with a tall companion at his side. 'Come on, Barry, let's get her. You stay there, young lady!' he growled menacingly. Suddenly it came to her.

'It was Billy who tied up my mum! And the other one – Barry – he was the postman who was trying to take my letter! But I didn't let him,' said Janey into the SPIV, not sure if G-Mamma was even able to hear.

Billy and Barry separated and moved in on her in a pincer movement that would leave Janey swatted against the seating plan like a butterfly specimen. She looked behind her, but Edna had deliberately piled some wooden crates across the exit and was now standing in front of them, shaking her head sorrowfully. Miss Rale had abandoned Uncle James and was gliding towards Janey, a silent predator. And next to her, in a shimmering dress, with long, blonde tresses curling over her shoulders like Goldilocks, was another woman. Or rather a girl. Was this the sister Miss Rale had mentioned earlier?

All this rattled through Janey's mind like machine-gun fire as she scanned the room for an escape. Should she try the Fleet-feet jump? The group was moving stealthily through the crowds, and crawling along on its long flat belly was Ariel's dog. Any moment now he'd be able to leap under the table and pounce on Janey's ankles. She was trapped, surrounded.

'Bratwurst!' shouted the Goldilocks girl, her hair flying back to reveal small, ice-white teeth as vicious as her dog's. 'Get her!'

'No!' began Janey, jumping desperately left, then right, trying to think, to get out. Her jumps activated the Fleet-feet pads: there was a small thud against the floor and she bounced up towards the ceiling.

As she left the ground a small furry bomb with fluorescent go-faster stripes and a beacon for a tail belted out from under the buffet table, quiff

179

quivering. Trouble the kitten skimmed across the floor like an Exocet missile, bounding low and fast through the space beneath Janey's feet. Fixing on his target, Trouble extended his legs and sank his claws deep into the neat round bottom of Bratwurst. The dog skittered, yelping, across the floor towards Goldilocks, but Trouble hung on to the dog's behind and they rocketed across the floor together, scattering guests in all directions. Leaping again towards Goldilocks, Bratwurst spun his back end around like an articulated lorry taking a sharp bend. Trouble had no option but to let go. The girl tripped over the dog, and Trouble flew through the air, crashing into Billy and Barry. Spinning, they banged into each other and fell to the floor, yowling even more loudly than the cat. The pile of spies snarled and spat as each animal struggled to be back at the other's throat.

In the confusion, Janey frantically considered her options. The unwitting guests were now picking up the Sinerlesse members and brushing them down. They would be after her again any minute, maddened now to a state of vicious fury. It was hopeless. Janey had no Girl-gauntlet, no G-Mamma, no Satispy, not even Uncle James to help her focus. All she had was her innate Spylet wit. And a kitten who looked like a zebra crossing.

Then Janey gasped. Uncle James might not be able to help. But there was another uncle who might be able to do something.

Racing back down the length of the table, Janey skidded to a halt where she had heard the voice before.

She pretended to bury her head in her hands in despair, then whispered frantically through her fingers. 'Uncle Sol! If you can hear me, help! Help me, please!'

And this time, Janey knew exactly where the voice was coming from. 'Sing for your supper, Janey, Sing!'

Janey couldn't stop to take in the fact that she had just had a conversation with a frozen swan. She leaped on to the table and clapped her hands.

19 tutu terrors

It was Janey Brown's worst nightmare come true.

She wasn't in her pink tutu, so that was something. But she was back-lit, wearing a transparent shower curtain, standing on a table in front of a huge, very confused audience. And now she was going to have to sing. She was going to have to entertain all these people with a voice even more unpleasant than Bratwurst's with Trouble's claws in his bum.

I can't! she thought. She couldn't see how singing was going to save her now, but she had to trust Uncle Solomon. Maybe he had a plan.

Two hundred pairs of eyes had swivelled in Janey's direction. Even the Sinerlesse crew froze on the spot.

Janey wanted to jump off the table and run away as fast as her Fleet-feet would carry her. But that wouldn't save her skin. And it certainly wouldn't save Uncle Solomon. And it wasn't something that Jane Blonde would ever do. Squaring her shoulders and standing as straight as she possibly could, Janey smiled nervously at the crowd in front of her.

'Um, hello!' she began lamely. Across the dance floor she spotted Uncle James, eyes bulging. She cleared her throat and started again.

'Hello, everyone! Erm, you won't know me, but my name is Janey, and I'm a very, very good friend of . . . of Bratwurst's.' Good friends with a dog? Oh well done, Janey, she thought. But a ripple of applause clattered around the ballroom; clearly most people here had no idea that Bratwurst was a small and evil canine.

'Well, as you all know, tonight is a very special night for Bratwurst, the St Earl's dog. That's why we're all here! Yes, it's a very special night for Bratwurst and his lovely owner, umm . . . Goldilocks! And Billy, there, and his Barry next to him. Miss R— I mean, Susan, in that lovely red dress. And Edna, who deserves a round of applause for all this fantastic food.'

As she spoke, Janey put her hands together. The audience applauded on cue as if they'd rehearsed it. 'And, so,' Janey shouted over the noise, 'I think we should sing that special celebration song that we all love so much!'

Everyone looked on expectantly. Janey wished she had G-Mamma here to make up a rap for her. But she didn't. So she smiled bravely, took a deep breath and sang.

'Happy birthday to you . . .' To her immense relief, nearly the whole room joined in immediately. 'Happy birthday to you! Happy birthday, dear Bratwurst. Happy birthday to you!'

Applause thundered into the roof of the

ballroom. The Sinerlesse members looked furious and started to move towards her, arms outstretched.

'Again!' Janey shouted. 'And . . . and let's give all of them the bumps!'

The Sinerlesse were helpless to retaliate as dozens of hands lifted them off their feet and started to bounce their horizontal bodies in time to the music. Janey could see that even Edna had been grabbed by the waiting staff and was now displaying her grey and red striped bloomers to the guests. She didn't have long. With a quick appraisal of the room, into the roof and up and down the trestle tables, she identified her means of escape.

'Oh, Uncle Sol, I really hope I haven't gone completely loopy,' she muttered, leaning over the ice swan. A thin laugh like wind chimes echoed around her head. Where had she heard that sound before?

The singing and bumping was coming to a halt and Goldilocks-girl was back on her feet. Quick as a flash, Janey leaned into the swan's hollowed-out wings and started pulling out the fizzing pineapples. Though the sparklers grazed against her body, her SPI-suit stopped her from feeling any pain, and she managed to clutch a dozen to her.

'Well done, everyone!' she shouted. 'And here's the finale!'

And with that, Janey started lobbing pineapples into the audience and all around her. Sparks arced through the air and sizzled against the food. One or two caught the tasselled edges of the tablecloths, where they began

to smoulder. A bunch of people, whose instant concentration would have impressed Uncle James, leaped for
the fire extinguishers and started squirting furiously. As
smoke, flames, foam and glittering sparks exploded
around the room, Janey ran a few steps back along the
table top towards the seating plan, still clutching one of
the sparkling pineapples.

Suddenly Goldilocks, her golden hair now tousled
and matted, elbowed her way out of the crowd and lunged
forward to grab Janey's dress.

Janey saw the shower curtain pull away from her
headscarf belt. She was now standing there in just her Jane
Blonde outfit. And it felt fantastic. It couldn't have been
further from the agony of her tutu nightmare. Her
assailant looked up with furious, narrowed eyes and
grabbed for Janey's foot with her hands – very familiar,
slender, neat little hands . . .

'You won't escape from me, you know,' screamed the
girl, her voice shrill. 'Don't you now know who I am?'

'Ariel!' cried Janey, stunned. 'You're Ariel.'

'That's right. And you're pathetic and sad. Just like
my sister said in one of her many notes about you: "If
Janey Brown was any more boring . . ."'

'Nooo!' Swelling with fury, Janey jumped and planted
a kick firmly in Ariel's ribs, sending her enemy sprawling
to the floor.

Ariel struggled to her feet. She now looked very
peculiar indeed, as her lustrous golden locks had slid
forward on to her face. Angrily she reached up and

pulled the wig off to reveal a small, razor-haired, delicate-featured young person.

'Freddie?' squeaked Janey in shock. '*You're* Ariel?'

The familiar face looked back at her furiously. And it all made sense. Freddie's strange, gruff voice that always sounded so forced, the way he'd reacted when he'd snagged his fingernail . . . the silver locket. Freddie was a girl!

'My name's Freda, not Freddie, you idiot, but now I'm Ariel. And you know what else? I'm your worst nightmare.'

But Janey just grinned and twirled the sparkler she was holding. 'No, you're not. I've just experienced the real live version of my worst nightmare. And actually, I feel fine. So now watch me be . . . what did the note say? So boring I'm invisible!'

Leaping beyond Ariel's clutches, Janey sprinted back down the table towards the ice swan.

'Hold on, Uncle Sol! I just hope these SPI-buys do what I think they do!'

Janey touched the glowing end of the sparkler first to one rocket-shaped hairslide, then to the other. As a riotous fizzing erupted next to her ears, she lowered her head and grabbed the wing-feathers of the swan. The hairslides blasted into action, whooshing deafeningly, and Janey felt her feet lift from the table with the rush of an aeroplane engine. Sparks and fire rushed over her shoulders as Janey and the swan flew along the tabletop, propelled by the two tiny rockets. Food flew into the audience as Janey steamed along like an express train, then launched into open space as the table ended, before crashing out in an explosion of glass and ice, through the ballroom window and into the open air.

As she clung to the ice swan, Janey sailed though the night sky, shaking her ponytail and whooping with joy. 'Yessss!' she shouted to the stars, ignoring the cries from the ballroom far below.

'Janey! Janey Brown! Get back here at once. What on earth am I going to tell your mother? Janeeeeeeey!'

ice-capades

Janey rode the ice swan like a toboggan, leaning into the curves and hurtling over the tightly packed snow. They had been racing across hillsides for several minutes before she spotted some buildings a couple of miles ahead. Janey jammed a foot into the snow, then, wrenching the swan round with all the strength she could muster, she turned its beak to face back up the hillside. To her great relief, the ice swan first slowed, then faltered, then stopped.

They were just above the buildings, which looked like barns or sheds. Pulling the swan along behind her, Janey used the Ultra-gogs as sensors. One building contained some horses and a cow; another straw. The smallest hummed as they approached it.

'It's a generator,' Janey read aloud from her Ultra-gogs.

'In there!' chimed the icy voice.

Janey pushed and heaved the swan through the large doors, then leaned against them, breathing heavily from the exertion.

'Closer!' whispered the voice. 'Closer, and leave me!'

Grunting and straining with all her might, Janey pushed the enormous ice sculpture to the rear of the barn, next to the generator, then headed back into the shadows outside. The wait was endless. She could hear strange creaks, groans and squelching sounds, and in the corner of her Ultra-gogs the heat sensor was pulsing with ever-increasing intensity.

'Are you all right?' she called out.

There was no answer. Clasping her knees to her chest, more in apprehension than with cold, she took deep breaths and waited, imagining the uproar back at the mansion. How long would it be before the Sinerlesse were back on their tail? Finally the barn door opened and a deep voice spoke into the darkness.

'Come in, Janey.'

Janey was shaking as she rose slowly to her feet and walked into the generator-building. A man was sitting on a bale of straw, dressed in some overalls that had been hanging in the shed. A shaft of moonlight fell through the crack in the open doorway on to his chiselled, handsome face.

Janey gasped. 'You're not Uncle Sol!'

The man looked confused. 'Aren't I? I should be – unless something has gone hideously wrong in the thaw-out. One can never be quite sure . . .'

'You don't look like Uncle Sol,' said Janey, confused. 'Uncle Sol has a round red face, with sticky-out ears and a bald head.' Not at all like you, thought Janey, taking in the man's tall, broad frame, and the strong face with its sharp blue eyes and thick dark hair.

'Oh, that Uncle Sol.' The man laughed, his weary face lighting up. 'The Sol's Lols picture. Well, I could hardly use a real picture of myself for the Sol's Lols logo, could I?'

'So,' Janey stammered, edging a little nearer, 'are you really my uncle Solomon?'

The man smiled at her, and a little piece of Janey's heart melted. 'Dear Janey,' he said, 'I hope I'm not too much of a disappointment, after all you've done for me in the last few weeks. I've put you into all sorts of danger. Unforgivable really. But I needed you to get involved—'

'No!' interrupted Janey. 'I don't mind! I mean, I'm glad you came to me. It's been incredible. But I don't really see how I've helped at all.'

Patting the bale next to him, Uncle Sol motioned to her to sit down. Even through her SPI-suit she could feel how cold he was, and there was a visible blue tinge to his skin. 'Where to start, Janey? Where to start?'

Janey thought for a moment. 'Well, for me it all started with G-Mamma.'

'G-Mamma? Who the . . . Oh, your godmother! Rosie! That's just the kind of name she would give herself.' Uncle Solomon chuckled and his blue eyes sparkled with laughter. 'Well, as you know, she is your SPI:KE. I started Solomon Polifical Investigations . . . oh, about the time you were born, I suppose. I wanted to carry on your father's good work. I've recruited

SPIs from all over the world. Only the best, mind you. We are a small and select organization. I only recruit people who were recommended to me by your dad, Janey. Or, of course,' he added, nudging Janey's arm, 'their children. Spylets.'

'So what G-Mamma said about Mum being Gina Bellarina, and Dad being a SPI too – that really is all true?'

Uncle Solomon waved a hand at Janey's outfit. 'Don't you feel it, Janey? Wasn't it perfectly evident the moment you were asked to do something that drew on your hidden resources, on the strengths you didn't even know you had?'

Janey knew it was true. She had felt it almost from the moment that she met G-Mamma. It was she, Janey, who had come up with a plan to save her mum. It was she who had solved her uncle Solomon's clues. It was she who had worked out the Sinerlesse Group's cover. And hadn't she just rescued herself and her uncle from their clutches?

Janey gazed up at her uncle and nodded.

'Good,' he continued. 'Well, some time ago I discovered something.'

'It's to do with the way the frog freezes, isn't it?' asked Janey, eyes wide.

'Yes, and more besides. Copernicus – your god-mother told you about him? – he asked me to take on a special project on behalf of the government. Project Crystal Clear. Basically, it was a study of how to preserve people by freezing them and then bringing them back to life. It's called cryogenics. As part of it, I started looking at the North American wood frog.' He paused for breath, panting slightly. 'Amazing creatures. Of course, there's been work on cryogenics before, lots of it. But from those frogs I learned something that would take it to a stage more advanced than ever before. And during my investigations I discovered something truly miraculous. Something frighteningly, catastrophically dangerous, if it fell into the wrong hands.'

A terrifying secret was about to be handed to her. Janey could feel it. 'I'm not sure I want to know, Uncle Sol!'

'I know, Janey. I understand how that feels. But I'm in danger. I won't let the secret be discovered by the Sinerlesse. So you have to destroy the files if I'm caught or killed. You're the one person in the world I would trust completely, Janey. You're family. And now you're a SPI. You're one of us.'

'But what about Mum? She's family, and she is . . . was . . . one of us too.'

Uncle Sol's eyes misted. 'Well, your father was very clear on two points. The first was that your mother should never be put in danger. So that you, Janey, would always have one parent to protect you and love you. Gina wouldn't be safe if she knew what was going on.'

For a long moment, Janey tried to imagine how different her life would have been if her mum hadn't always been there for her, to pick her up from nursery and school and chess club, to tuck her into bed at night, to talk to her about homework and hobbies.

'I understand. G-Mamma sort of told me that too. That my dad wanted me to have a normal life. But everything's changed now, hasn't it? Tell me everything, Uncle Sol.'

'I can't do that. The knowledge would put you in too much danger. I just need you to destroy—'

'No!' said Janey, more loudly than she'd intended. 'You have to tell me everything now. You got me into this in the first place. Tell me!'

Solomon sighed and shook his head. 'I only got you involved because I'd sent you something important, something—'

But before Solomon could explain, they heard people at the door.

'They're in here!' Ariel's voice rang piercingly.

Seconds later, the door banged open.

'Solomon Brown. We're very pleased to meet you at long last.'

Silhouetted against the night sky were Miss Rale, Edna, Billy and Barry. Before them, tiny but strangely terrifying, was Freda Lear: Ariel. Her ball gown had been ripped off to reveal a spysuit very similar to Janey's, but it was a darker grey with maroon edging. Without her long wig she looked much more like the Freddie that Janey remembered.

'We knew you'd be here, Solomon.' Ariel circled them slowly. 'We knew that if the Spylet was in any danger you'd turn up to rescue her. She was obviously heading straight for a meeting with you when she made her little rocket-powered table-top escape. And here you are.'

Solomon glowered, and Janey moved a little closer to him, thinking furiously.

'I mean, you really did leave so many clues! And I'm very good at puzzles. Sloppy work, Solomon! Calling your niece to a meeting at the Sol's Lols headquarters? After I intercepted the letter, it took us a little while to work out that the message was on the envelope. And the wood-frog diagram. Did you think we wouldn't be able to solve it? I think you underestimated our powers of deduction, Solomon. You thought we were simple!'

Uncle Solomon laughed. 'I never considered the Sinerlesse Group to be simple, Ariel. Devious. Dangerous, perhaps. But simple? Never.'

'You hadn't even worked out who we were! Although the name was pretty good. "St Earl's Sanitation and Security Enterprises".' Ariel looked quite smug. 'Took me a little while to make that up.'

'I had my suspicions. But I wasn't able to warn you, Janey.'

'I worked it out for myself, Uncle Sol. Dingbats! You've been training me up for a long time.'

He smiled at her before turning back to Ariel. 'Now why don't you tell me who leaked my project to you?'

Miss Rale started to emit a screeching laugh. 'Solomon, Solomon, Solomon. Your brain must have melted if you think we give up information like that. Now, if you had some SPIT, of course, we'd all squawk like

194

constipated parrots. Tell you everything. Wouldn't we, Janey?'

Janey looked at the floor uncomfortably, but her uncle reached an arm around her shoulders. 'SPIT? You're a bit behind the times. I sent Janey SPIT for her fourth birthday!'

'The perfume!' said Janey out loud. So that was why her mother had burbled on relentlessly when she'd tried it.

Ariel sneered, her sharp little teeth winking in the torchlight. 'Well, that was then, Brown, and this is now. And I'd say we've caught up, wouldn't you?'

Janey was scared. They were trapped in the barn with five people between them and the door, which as far as she could see was the only way out. Beside her, Uncle Solomon radiated confidence, but Janey could hear the tiny whistle in his breath that hinted at the transformation he had just undergone. How could he be so calm? They could be killed at any moment.

'But if you needed me to bring you to Uncle Sol, why did you try to kill me? The soap, the bucket . . .'

Her old teacher turned her sweet face towards her. 'We weren't trying to kill you, Janey. If we'd wanted to kill you, we would have done. And anyway, the bucket was meant for Alfie Halliday. We worked out exactly who he is.'

Janey frowned. Who was he?

'But no,' continued Miss Rale, 'we achieved exactly what we wanted. You and your mother got frightened, she got you out of the clutches of Rosie Biggenham next door and you became convinced you were the only Spylet who could find your uncle and sort this whole thing out. Then you really would step up your clumsy efforts. And look – that's exactly what you did! Gold star for you, Janey Brown! You'll get a very good report this term. Ha! Ha ha! Ha ha!'

As she watched the teacher she had once adored racked with evil laughter, Janey felt a stinging behind her eyes. Ariel was smirking at her unkindly.

'Hey, do you know what else, Janey?' said Ariel. 'Do you know why I pretended to be a boy? Because we know you so well, that's why! Because we could see that as a girl I would be so stunning in comparison to mousy Janey Brown that you would be too threatened to make friends with me. But a little boy, well, that was no problem, was it? Then there were the notes Susan wrote about you – they really helped turn you into the school freak. Drove you to make friends with the only person who was remotely nice to you. Helpful Freddie. I mean, me! You're a sad, sad creature.'

'Leave Janey alone,' said her uncle suddenly. 'She didn't even know she was a Spylet until a few days ago, and look at everything she's managed to do in that time. No doubt you've had a lifetime of plotting and evil, Ariel, but Janey's already outwitted you on several occasions. Remember Scotland, and the ball. She's made you look foolish, Ariel. Janey is a hundred times the Spylet that you are. And a million times the person.'

At that, Ariel's pretty face screwed up with rage. She

lifted her hand, complete with Girl-gauntlet, and pointed accusingly at Solomon. 'And who made me this way? Who poured this evil into our family and made us so vengeful? You did! You Browns!'

Janey looked in astonishment at Uncle Solomon, and he stared back, equally confused.

'We did nothing to you, Ariel.'

'You did. It was your buffoon of a brother – your darling pops, Janey. He killed my parents!'

real earls

'You're the children of Reg and Lally Baron,' said Uncle Solomon, nodding slowly.

'At last!' snapped Ariel. 'Not quick on the uptake, you Browns, are you? A Baron is roughly the same as an Earl. All our names are anagrams of Earl. How could you miss it?'

Uncle Sol shrugged easily. 'I suppose I could never have imagined Baron's family turning into something so evil. Anyway, it was an accident, Ariel. Boz and Reg were carrying out an experiment together when it went wrong and the whole laboratory was burned down. Nothing could have been done to save Reg.'

'Lies!' spat Ariel. 'Then my mother died giving birth to me. She had nothing to live for after she lost her husband. My brothers and sisters hate you Browns –' Susan, Barry and Billy nodded – 'but not as much as I do. I have never known either of my parents, and it's your fault. I've made it my life's goal to avenge their deaths. And who would think a pretty little thing like me could lead an entire organization? People tend to trust children

you know, let them overhear things they really shouldn't
. . . I was the perfect choice to take control of the
project intended to Wipe. You. Out.'

Solomon sighed. 'Your father would be devastated to
hear this, Ariel. Reg was committed to the work he and
Boz were doing together. He was a good man – it would
hurt him to see what his death created.'

The Sinerlesse siblings glared at Solomon and Janey.
Only Edna allowed a tear to trickle down the dome of her
cheek.

Ariel pointed the stun-gas finger of her Girl-gauntlet
in Solomon's face. 'Enough. You know nothing about my
father. It was your brother who knew him well, and it was
your brother who killed him. And seeing as you'll be dead
soon I might as well tell you that it was Copernicus who
handed us the perfect excuse to come after you. And now
we know the secret you have been trying to hide from us.
So you can stop playing for time. Take us right now to
where Boz Brown is, and we can make sure we're rid of
the murderous pig. And then, of course, we shall deal with
the pair of you.'

'My dad?' blurted Janey. Something red flashed in the
corner of her Ultra-gogs.

'Oh,' said Ariel in mock pity, shooting a disparaging
glance at Uncle Solomon. She looked every bit as
ferocious as Bratwurst. 'Haven't you told her, Solomon?
That you have her daddy tucked away in a deep freeze
somewhere? Cryogenically preserved. Well, if you
think you're going to bring your brother back to life

some day so you can all play happy families again, then I'm afraid you're terribly deluded!'

With that she nodded to the group behind her, who moved in to seize Janey and her uncle. Janey's head was spinning – what did Ariel mean? Was her dad really still alive somewhere? It was all Janey wanted to think about, but she had to stay focused on the danger she was in right now. As she was dragged out of the barn, she read the scarlet lettering on her Ultra-gogs. '"Cryogenics – the science of preservation through freezing, experimental at this stage." Ref. *Cantab Dictionary*, 1999.'

Project Crystal Clear had been about cryogenics, it was true. But Uncle Solomon had discovered more than that. He'd surpassed the boundaries of known cryogenics. Janey just didn't yet know how.

And neither did the Sinerlesse Group. They didn't have a clue that Uncle Solomon had actually *been* the ice swan. They thought he'd been waiting in the barn for Janey to arrive. They had completely misunderstood Solomon's secret and were looking for the wrong thing. Uncle Sol had progressed far beyond preserving bodies.

Ariel had no idea.

Jane Blonde had the advantage.

Swallowing down her excitement, Janey carefully checked out the location of each of their captors. Billy and Barry had taken hold of her uncle and were dragging him along behind her, past the barn full of straw. Miss Rale and Edna had each seized one of Janey's arms, while just ahead of her Ariel led the way with the narrow beam of light from her Girl-gauntlet.

It was perfect. With a sniff, Janey made her lip wobble slightly, as if she was trying bravely not to cry. Then she let out a small sob.

Edna squeezed her arm. 'Look, Janey,' she said kindly, 'I'm sure you didn't know what you were letting yourself in for. I'll talk to Freda and ask her to be nice to you. Can't promise anything, mind you.'

'It's not that, Edna,' whispered Janey with a sniff. 'It's just the thought that my father might be alive and I'll never get to meet him. I mean, maybe your son . . . your Reg . . . is alive too. Wouldn't it be awful, to know he was alive, preserved somewhere, and you never got to see him again?'

Edna's eyes clouded with doubt, then tears. 'I never thought of that! Oh, do you think he might be? My darling Reginald. Oh my!' And with that Edna stopped dead and slapped her hand dramatically to her heart, sobbing noisily.

'Oh, Granny, get a grip,' said Miss Rale unkindly.

Janey only had a few precious moments. The group had stopped, with everyone looking back to see what was upsetting Edna. Just as Janey had hoped, Ariel came right up to her grandmother, who reached out her hands to her youngest granddaughter.

There was no time to waste. Janey shoved hard with her right hip, sending Edna sprawling into the snow. In the same movement she grabbed Ariel's

Girl-gauntlet, pointed it at Miss Rale and squeezed the little finger hard. Stun-gas sprayed directly into Miss Rale's face and she slumped to the floor as if she'd been shot. Ariel was baying and squirming, but Janey was too strong for her. She wrapped her arms around Ariel from behind and hoped desperately that her enemy was wearing Fleet-feet. She lifted the smaller girl as high as she could and then dropped her on to the ground. With a bang, Ariel's feet exploded into life and she was flung several metres into the air. Screaming loudly and with all limbs flapping, she tumbled down the hillside.

Uncle Solomon struggled to get away from the men, but they had too tight a grip. Janey ran straight towards them, pulling on the Girl-gauntlet she had ripped from Ariel's hand. She pointed her index finger and squeezed as hard as she could into Billy's eyes.

'Not again, you . . . you . . .' he screeched, flapping at his face as ink blasted into his eyeballs. 'My eyes!'

With one arm freed, Uncle Solomon spun Barry around and pushed him into Billy. Careering into each other, the two men fell to the ground and lay stunned, groaning loudly.

Meanwhile, Ariel was back on her feet and running back up the hillside towards them.

'Can you ride a horse, Uncle Sol?' shouted Janey, grabbing his arm and sprinting towards one of the barns.

He laughed. 'I can do anything – I'm a SuperSPI, aren't I? Let's go!'

And less than a minute later, just as Ariel reached the

barn with her grandmother panting along behind her, Janey and Uncle Solomon burst out of the small back door, whooping and laughing and clinging on for all they were worth to an enormous galloping carthorse.

spi surprises

The horse was wild with joy at being released from its stall and galloped across the open countryside with what felt like more speed and nearly as much height as the Satispy. Janey, encircled by her uncle's arms, lowered her head and entwined her fingers still further into the horse's mane. She felt completely exhilarated. But after a few miles she could sense that her uncle was beginning to weaken.

'Find the crossroads at Allerton, Janey. We'll get help there.'

'OK!' According to her Ultra-gogs, Allerton was just a mile or so away. 'Uncle Sol, you have to tell me more about your discovery. And I need to know what happened to my dad.'

'You know Ariel has got it wrong?' answered Solomon.

'Yeah, I don't think she realized you actually *were* the swan. But you really did end up being turned into an ice lolly!'

'Exactly, Janey!' her uncle said. 'Just think about that.

For a long time, scientists have tried to preserve things – organs, bodies and so on – by cooling them very quickly to minus 200 degrees Celsius in liquid nitrogen. But that causes all sorts of damage that can't be put right.'

'Like the frogs that were frozen and got snapped.'

'Exactly. So I worked out how to freeze things to a low temperature but over a much longer time frame, with no damage to the subject. It started with animals. And I've discovered it can be done with humans too. I've done it to myself, and to one other person – a very brave SPI who insisted on being a guinea pig for me. And the results were amazing. What I discovered was just . . . just incredible really,' he went on. 'But even that was only the beginning. My experiments developed and I found a way to transform a person into any frozen form. Imagine that, Janey. My SPI colleague and I tried it on each other, and it works amazingly well. Once we became ice, pure ice, we could be moulded into any shape.'

'Like frozen swimming pools, Uncle Sol?'

'Exactly. I was in there with you that evening. You did everything right.' He smiled proudly at her. 'When I realized the Sinerlesse were closing in, I put myself through the Crystal Clarification Process. I had hidden in my office. Because I wasn't forming into a particular shape, for which you need an assistant, I was able to get myself on to the surface of the pool and transform into a simple layer of ice.'

Janey remembered the photograph she had taken in her uncle's office. 'You went through the tube!' He nodded. 'But what happens when the pool melts,' she continued, 'or if someone slurps you up from their drink?'

'Well, it's a very, very complex cellular activity. If the freezing process is carried out correctly, each cell is tagged and becomes a crystal. Those frogs taught me that previous attempts at cryogenics hadn't worked because the subjects were frozen too quickly. It has to be painstakingly slow. Then, after you've melted again, a magnetic field draws all the cells back into their original form. But there is always risk involved. Look what happened this time.' Her uncle held his hand in front of Janey's face, and she saw that his thumb and half his forefinger were missing.

She shuddered. 'You're so brave, Uncle Sol.'

'Brave? I'm not so sure. I'm almost sorry I discovered it, Janey. I thought it would be of huge benefit to SPIs. Just imagine the meetings, the planning sessions you could get into in this way and never be detected. You could clink around in someone's water jug, listening to every plot they're hatching. At outdoor locations you could lie like a frozen puddle, finding out what your target was up to. And, provided you have the equipment with you, all your cells can be drawn together again from wherever you ended up. It's spying supreme. But in the wrong hands . . .'

'Like Ariel's,' said Janey grimly.

'Quite. Evil-minded people could discover secrets, infiltrate all sorts of decision-making forums and create havoc. They could even freeze their enemies!'

'And turn them into ice swans?'

'Whatever they wanted. They could turn them into snow-globes and keep them in the freezer. The sculptor – the creator – has the key to all that power.'

'And is that power what the Sinerlesse Group wants?'

Uncle Solomon patted the horse to slow it down. He leaned towards Janey's ear. 'I don't think they have any idea what it is they seek. They mentioned Copernicus, but thank God I never gave him access to my complete files. Even he doesn't know the extent of what I've discovered. He must be paying the Sinerlesse to track down my secret for him – which is clever of him, given their personal grievance against me. Revenge is a dangerous motive, Janey. But of course the Sinerlesse don't really have a clue what I've discovered. And they're wrong about your father . . .'

Janey's heart lurched again. So her father wasn't alive. She desperately wanted to know more, but there was no time now. The Ultra-gogs beeped, telling them they had reached Allerton. Unfortunately the sound went off right in the horse's ear; it reared up and pranced madly, throwing both Janey and her uncle to the ground. They landed with a crash in a hedgerow.

'Uncle Sol, are you all right?' shouted Janey.

A voice boomed out of the darkness above them. 'Could you make a bit more noise, Brown? I'm not sure the Sinerlesse Group has *quite* pinpointed where you are.'

Alfie Halliday towered over Janey, extending

a hand to help her up. Glancing nervously at Uncle Solomon, she took his brief nod as approval and allowed herself to be dragged to her feet.

'Told you to be careful who you made friends with,' he said with a huge grin.

'I . . . you . . .' Janey was staggered. Ariel's earlier comment about Alfie was beginning to make sense. 'I think I know what you were hiding under your stairs. It's a SPI-lab, isn't it?'

'Oh, you did see that?' Alfie looked amused. 'Better SPI than I thought, then.'

'Don't be a pest, Al. She's been through quite enough this evening without you provoking her as well.' Stunned, Janey watched as Mrs Halliday appeared behind him.

She turned to Janey's uncle. 'Well, Mr Brown, I'm glad you're not a swan any more. You were very slippery to handle at that ball. Alfie nearly dropped you!'

'Maisie.' Hugging her warmly, Uncle Solomon laughed. 'Thanks for waiting. And thank heavens Rosie told you what was happening, once she'd discovered who you are.'

Mrs Halliday grinned, showing her jagged teeth. 'Well, she was very surprised to see me out of retirement, and it's all been a bit rushed. I've told her you alerted us as you went into hiding, but that was all. We didn't even have enough time to jump in the Wower – we just had to grab what we could! But Rosie managed to let me know the essentials, once Janey SPIVed across the information about the ball and St Earl's.'

'We can't have much time,' said Alfie. 'Let's get going.'

Janey watched with amazement as Alfie and his mother pulled a large square suitcase out from under a pile of leaves. Opening it up, Alfie took four wheels out of the case and attached two to one side, while his mother did the same at the other side. He then reached forward and pulled something, and a steering wheel sprang into place, bristling with instruments and camera gadgetry. At the same time, four inflatable seats unfolded themselves drunkenly, and within seconds Alfie stood back to usher them into the four-seater go-kart he had just created.

'Where to?' asked Alfie as his mother lowered her tall frame into the bucket seat next to him.

Hesitating for a moment, Solomon weighed up a few options. 'Let's head for the lab near Winchester. I can refreeze there before they find me again.'

Alfie nodded. 'Shake a leg, Blonde,' he said, pointing towards the back of the little car.

She took the seat next to her uncle and they set off with a huge jolt. Janey clutched at her throat in alarm. 'Oh no! I've lost my SPIV!' she said. 'I must have dropped it somewhere. How am I going to get in touch with G-Mamma?'

'Chill out, Blonde,' said Alfie. 'We can protect you.'

'And why would you do that? I thought you hated me,' snapped Janey.

'Nah, you're all right. I was just trying to toughen you up,' said Alfie.

As they continued to career around trees and

skitter through streams and brooks, Janey turned to her uncle. 'Alfie's a Spylet too, isn't he? So both his parents were SPIs?'

'Of course – he's Al Halo!' said Uncle Solomon. 'Maisie was one of your mother's colleagues. SPI-name: Halo. We wondered whether your mother would remember her when you went round for tea. It was a bit of a test. I'm glad to say she didn't.'

'And Alfie's father?'

'Yes, he was a SPI too. But his work has taken him away from his family . . .'

Just like me, thought Janey. No wonder Alfie had been so snappy when Janey had asked about the postcards.

'You can trust them, Janey,' continued Solomon. 'Maisie is the only other person who knows my secret. I have trusted her completely since the beginning. And she's done a lot for you already – she even made you a makeshift escape kit when she found out the Sinerlesse Group had your mother on the roof.'

'My PE bag!' Janey shouted.

'I'm terribly sorry, Janey,' said Mrs Halliday earnestly. 'I had no idea Miss Rale was a fake, although we thought there was something funny about Freddie from quite early on.'

'I did, you mean!' said Alfie. 'Weirdo. Something not quite right about that boy.'

'He's not a boy . . . he's a girl!' said Janey. 'A girl called Freda. But she prefers to go by another name:

Ariel. Little Freddie Lear is actually the leader of the Sinerlesse!'

'No!' said Alfie and his mother in unison, before bursting into a heated spat about who had suspected what and why.

Janey's uncle grinned. 'They'll look after you, if you don't end up looking after them! Now, it looks like we've arrived.'

Ahead of them stood the enormous gates of a wildlife park. Huge models of wild animals lined the narrow country road. Alfie pressed a button on the steering wheel and a laser beam shot out, making contact with a tiny red dot at the base of the wrought-iron gates. Noiselessly the gates slid apart to let the go-kart zip through.

Janey could hear the howls of animals calling, and her scalp prickled under her ponytail. Alfie guided the go-kart expertly along the paths of the park, but her intuition told Janey where they were heading.

'We're going to the Amphibian House, aren't we, Uncle Sol?'

His eyes sparking with admiration through the darkness, Uncle Solomon nodded. 'Despite what G-Mamma may have told you, sometimes the most obvious place is the one the enemy least expects. And where else would you find North American wood frogs? Well done, Blonde. You're doing well.'

Inside, Janey was beaming with pride, but she tried to look as though she was not in the least overawed as Alfie rocketed around a corner on two wheels and pulled up in front of a large, low building with a screeching handbrake turn.

'Pest!' said Mrs Halliday disapprovingly as she struggled, wind-swept, from the go-kart.

Janey stood up and helped her uncle, who had been leaning on her more and more heavily as the journey progressed. In single file, the four SPIs approached the door of the Amphibian House.

Reaching up to a picture of an Australian tree frog, Solomon pressed one of its red eyeballs and the door appeared to evaporate before them. 'SPI-door. Only SPIs know how to get in – or out. You're one of us now, Janey.'

As they stepped further inside, the tropical heat of the house engulfed them.

'How could anything freeze in here?' Janey asked.

Beckoning to them to follow, Uncle Solomon walked over to a cylindrical glass display case in the centre of the Amphibian House. It was filled with North American wood frogs, alive but lethargic in the sweltering heat. The glass slid apart before them to create an opening.

'Do we have to get in with them?' As much as she had endured lately, Janey didn't fancy climbing into a glass cylinder with a bunch of slimy frogs.

Alfie snorted. 'Yep! In you go, Blonde!' he said, and with a firm hand he shoved her inside.

Once she was inside the cylinder Janey realized that the frogs were simply holographic images, projected on to the glass. The tube was empty – Janey had stepped on to a cushion of air and was suspended inside the glass tube

like something in a specimen jar. After a long hovering
moment, there was an enormous sucking sound and she
shot down the cylinder into what seemed like the depths
of the earth.

She tumbled out when she reached the bottom,
followed almost immediately by Alfie, Mrs Halliday and
her uncle. They were in an enormous white SPI-lab,
identical in style to G–Mamma's but about twenty times as
big. There were cupboards around the outside and a
Wower in one corner. Laboratory benches straddled the
middle of the room, and in another corner was an
enormous bow-fronted freezer.

And there, sitting in front of the freezer on a tall stool,
looking for all the world as though she was about to
entertain them with a song, was Ariel. Instead of a
microphone, however, she held a small bronze pistol. And
it was pointing directly at Janey.

frozen with fear

'Took your time, didn't you? No Satispy to whizz you over here, huh?' snarled Ariel.

The colour drained from Janey's face. 'But how did you know? How did you . . .'

Ariel lifted up her other hand. From her fingers dangled a horrible chunky necklace which Janey recognized immediately as her lost SPIV. She cringed as she heard G-Mamma's breathless voice.

'Blonde-girl, I'm getting there as fast as I can. You should be at the Wildlife Park by now – is he there? Have you found your uncle? Talk to me, honey-child!'

Ariel grinned evilly. 'I think you've done all the talking you're going to do for quite a while. G-Mamma! What a fool! Your G-Mamma told me everything – and she doesn't even know it! Now into the freezer!' she barked. 'All of you. Into the freezer!'

Just before she slammed the huge door shut, Ariel cocked her head to one side. For a moment she looked like a sweet little girl. 'Now don't forget: as soon as you decide to tell me where Boz Brown's frozen body is, I'll let you out. Or at least I'll think about letting you out. And in the meantime, I'm just going to turn this freezer up to HIGH. Help you think things through. You know how much I like to be helpful, don't you, Janey? Shout out when you're ready. Bye!'

'I'm sorry! I'm so sorry!' Janey turned helplessly to the three people captured with her. 'I lost the SPIV and it was still activated. I led her to you!'

'No, you didn't, Janey,' said Solomon carefully. 'And your godmother was only trying to help. She was looking after you, as she is meant to.'

As Maisie Halliday looked on, tapping her razor teeth thoughtfully, Alfie was working his way around the walls of the freezer. The whiteness of the walls was dazzling and Janey was glad that her Ultra-gogs had instantly darkened to provide some screen from the glare.

'Temperature,' she said. The Ultra-gogs screen flashed two degree Celsius. Then it flickered and changed to one degree. Zero. It was falling fast.

'There's no way out of here,' said Alfie, not sounding in the least perturbed. 'It's completely sealed, apart from that tiny hole in the door which appears to be the lock.'

'How can you sound so cheerful about it?' Janey felt like throwing herself at the walls, ranting and wailing like a mad girl in a padded cell.

'Well, you know, look who we're with!' Alfie pointed to Uncle Solomon, who had slid down the wall and was sitting with his head in his hands. 'If you're going to be frozen with someone, then who better than Solomon

Brown? We can be frozen, then shaped into something that can get through the lock or whatever, can't we, Solomon?'

Janey caught the harrowed look that passed between her uncle and Mrs Halliday before he turned to Alfie and Janey with pained eyes. 'Unfortunately, Al, all the shaping equipment is on the other side of the door.'

Janey groaned. 'She thinks if she threatens to freeze all of us, Uncle Sol will tell her where my father is.'

Her uncle nodded. 'But that's not possible, because there is no Boz to find.'

'The temperature's falling too fast, Uncle Sol. We're down at minus fifteen degrees already.'

'We'll die of hypothermia. So much for my ground-breaking discoveries! They won't help us when we're freezing at this rate. This is nothing like the other times we've frozen, M-Maisie.'

Mrs Halliday shuddered. 'No. Just l-lost some b-b-bits of my teeth that time.'

'M-my guinea p-p-pig,' stammered Solomon. 'Bravest of SP-SPIs. And she's kept my secret all this time.' Janey stared in amazement at Mrs Halliday, who smiled back weakly. She was obviously losing strength by the minute.

Janey could feel her own system slowly closing down too. Her body and right hand, protected by the SPI-suit and Ariel's Girl-gauntlet, were managing to stay quite warm, but her face and left hand were rigid with cold. Her ears were stinging and burning as icy air bit into them, and already her lips felt as though they might seal together.

Alfie was faring the best, but even he was starting to slap his arms with slower and slower movements, his head lolling forward as cold air filled his lungs. Mrs Halliday was trying to take off her coat and pass it to Alfie, but was shivering so violently that she couldn't get her arms out of the sleeves, while Solomon remained slumped on the floor, trying to resist as little as possible to conserve his energy.

'M-minus twenty. Twenty-three. Twenty-f-f-five.' An aching coldness now churned in the pit of her stomach. 'Keep moving! Must . . . keep moving!'

'Janey, if . . .' Uncle Solomon's voice was barely a whisper. 'The files . . . I told you before . . . must be destroyed, if I d-d-don't survive.'

'Don't s-s-say things like that! We will g-get out!' stammered Janey.

'S-save your strength, Janey.' Mrs Halliday nodded over to her son, tears freezing instantly on her lashes. 'You and Alfie might make it.'

Tears burned behind Janey's nose. It was hopeless. The only way out was through the locked door. And the key was on the other side, in Ariel's hand. Yet, even though her mind felt caged by icicles, Janey refused to give up. And suddenly she remembered something.

Shaking violently, she made her way over to the door. It was coated with a thin layer of ice. By feeling around with her Girl-gauntleted hand, she located the tiny lock. It was minuscule, barely big enough for a key any larger than a darning needle.

'Wh-what are you d-d-d-doing?' asked Alfie.

'Un-l-locking the door.' Janey hoped she'd managed to sound confident enough to give her friends and her uncle some hope.

Breathing heavily, Janey reached across with her numb left hand and removed the Girl-gauntlet. Then slowly, aware they might shatter with cold if she dropped them, Janey reached up to her solid ponytail and drew out the keys to her suitcase and to the en-suite bathroom at Uncle James's. The door key was much too big. But the other was tiny, though not tiny enough.

Janey laid the Girl-gauntlet on the icy floor and gently placed the little key on top. Then, using the bigger key as a chisel to grind the edges of the smaller one, Janey forced her rigid hands to chip away. One wrong move might snap the brittle metal completely. No matter how much Janey wanted to rush, she had to force herself to be slow, take her time.

'Focus, Janey!' she told herself.

It seemed to take forever, and while she worked Janey could hear her fellow SPIs' breathing growing irregular, more laboured. Finally she held up the suitcase key. It gleamed like a shard of glass in the harsh refrigerator glare.

'Tiny,' said Janey. Now it just might fit.

Rising stiffly to her feet, Janey pressed one Ultra-gogged eye to the lock, trying to make out the shape of the grooves within. She made a couple of tiny adjustments with the laser in the Girl-gauntlet, and took a deep breath.

Her uncle lifted his head just enough to see what she was doing.

'Let me!' he mouthed. 'If it works, she m-might shoot straight away.'

But Janey shook her head. He was close to death. The others were not much better. The only one with enough strength to face the enemy was Jane Blonde.

Shivering, she put the key into the lock and turned.

24 revelations

As the key turned the lock mechanism, there was a tiny noise like a mouse gnashing its teeth. Janey slid silently to the floor so that she lay outstretched. Then, reaching out both her hands, she made contact with the door and shoved.

The door creaked open. With a cry of astonishment and rage Ariel realized what was happening, but she was too late. Janey gave another firm push and there was a clunk as the heavy door ploughed into Ariel's stool, sending her clattering across the laboratory. Grabbing the stool from where it had fallen, Janey wedged the freezer door open and flung herself across the open space. She managed to roll behind the laboratory bench just as Ariel recovered herself and let loose with her pistol. A shot whistled past Janey's ear; she looked around desperately as Ariel got to her feet.

The shrill little voice echoed around the laboratory. 'Oh, don't worry, Brown. I'm not wasting any more bullets on you. I'll save these for your uncle.'

Janey poked her head around the bench and saw Ariel

brush herself down, then make her way deliberately towards the freezer door. What should she do? Leaping to her feet, she stepped out from behind the bench.

'Why my uncle? It's me you should be after!' Amazed at how strong her own voice sounded, Janey took another step forward. Ariel spun round and pointed the pistol directly at her. She was no more than ten metres away, as terrifying and vicious as a cornered mink.

'I just said it's Solomon I want, not you. You were only ever a way to entice him out of hiding,' said Ariel.

Janey shook her head. 'No. You want Boz. You think he's been frozen, preserved somewhere cryogenically until Sol works out how to thaw him out. And you want to make sure Boz is dead, like your parents. You think you've discovered Sol's great secret. But –' and she tried a scornful laugh – 'do you really think it would be something as old hat as cryogenics? I mean, *everyone* knows about cryogenics. You must be as dumb as you look, Goldilocks. That's not what my uncle's secret is. It's much, much bigger than that.'

'No, Janey!' Solomon cried from within the freezer. Ariel swivelled towards the freezer door and then back to Janey, two hands on the pistol now. She steadied it and took aim.

'I have to, Uncle Sol!' Janey shouted. She looked Ariel straight in the eyes. 'I'll tell you the secret, and you can sell it for millions. You'll have the power you crave. You'll be unstoppable. But you have to promise to let us go.'

'OK.' She heard the safety catch being pulled

back as Ariel curled her lip in a furious hiss. 'But if it's not a big enough secret, you die. What is it?'

And Janey, gulping, took a deep breath and told the biggest whopper she could imagine. 'The secret is . . . reincarnation! Solomon has discovered how to reincarnate people. They die as one person and come back as another.'

Ariel's eyes widened with amazement. 'It . . . it's not possible! It can't be!'

'Come on, Ariel,' mocked Janey. 'You know what an amazing scientist my uncle is. You can't imagine he'd be inventing a process that so many other people have already worked on, do you?'

'But Copernicus told us that Project Crystal Clear is about cryogenics!'

'Well, it seems my uncle wasn't the only one that Copper Knick . . . I mean Copernicus was double-crossing,' said Janey.

Ariel was trying to sound calm and masterful but it was obvious that what Janey had said had unsettled her. 'So not cryogenics. Reincarnation.' Her eyes hardened. 'Copernicus must have realized Solomon had gone further with his experiments and sent us to bring him in. He must want this information for himself. That's why he sent *us* after Solomon. He knew the history between my family and the Browns, so he sought us out. He used the Sinerlesse! I knew he'd sunk pretty low, turning on Solomon's Polifdcational Investigations, but this . . . this is indescribable. So you say it's you I'm after, Brown!

What do you mean? Who are you? Are you some reincarnation?'

Smiling as confidently as she could with the barrel of a pistol pointing straight at her, Janey opened her arms wide. 'Do you really need to ask that question, Ariel? You know! You know who I am. I told you I'm the one you're looking for. I'm Boz. Boz Brilliance Brown.'

Although she was shaking inside with a fear far greater than any she had ever known, Janey looked steadily at Ariel. With a slightly unsteady hand, Ariel aimed the gun directly at Janey's chest.

'Well. You've made me chase you a long, long way, Boz Brown,' Ariel whispered. 'But now the chase is over. Now I can put an end to you forever. As you did to my parents.'

And as Janey gritted her teeth and the gun exploded, a thousand things happened at once. A ball of fire seemed to go straight through Janey, blasting her backwards across the laboratory. Banging her head on the corner of a bench, she lifted her hands to her chest to find the hole, then slumped to the floor, sure death must be just seconds away.

There was another bang as Alfie, almost fully recovered, barged his way out of the freezer and high-kicked Ariel, who fell to the floor. As the pistol left her fingers, Alfie kicked it backwards, and his mother, stiff but alive, scooped it up and turned it swiftly on Ariel. In the same moment, whooshing sounds came from the entry cylinder behind them, and Miss Rale's voice could be heard saying, 'Look who I've found! Can't leave her precious godchild alone! Hey, what's going on . . . Oof!'

G-Mamma splurged from the cylinder, whipped round and smacked Miss Rale over the head with her SPIV, which was the size of a small coconut. As Miss Rale dropped to the ground Alfie hurried over and tied her hands behind her, dragging her over to where Mrs Halliday was training the pistol on Ariel. Meanwhile, with an agility that amazed Janey, G-Mamma flung herself to the floor, rolled over a couple of times and wedged herself under the bottom of the entry cylinder. Her wobbling flesh sealed it closed, creating a massive vacuum of air which simmered in the tube beneath Billy and Barry, who had no idea their exit was blocked. The cries of the two Sinerlesse members echoed through the SPI-lab as they were blasted up, up through the roof of the Amphibian House, before plummeting back down to land with two almighty splashes.

'That'll be the alligator pool,' said G-Mamma. 'Hope those crocs are hungry!'

From above, Janey could make out the voice of Edna wailing, 'I never wanted any of this, you know! Reg wouldn't have liked it! That Lally was always a bad influence. Stop it, Freda! Stop being such a naughty girl. I want it all to sto-ho-hop!'

Astonishingly, Janey felt as though she was able to sit up and go and check on her uncle. She looked down at herself. There was no hole, not even a dent. A slightly darker area on the silver of her SPI-suit was the only sign that anything had hit her at all.

'Bullet-proof!' Janey said. 'Of course!'

She got slowly to her feet as G-Mamma rose majestically from under the entry cylinder, suddenly looking every wonderful inch a superSPI.

'G-Mamma, I'm so pleased to see you!' Gulping back tears, Janey sped across the enormous room towards her godmother and flung herself into a bosomy embrace. 'How did you know where to find us?'

'Well, baby-mine,' said G-Mamma, almost blushing under her heavy make-up, 'the SPIV was still activated when your uncle mentioned Allerton. I figured the Wildlife Park was where he was headed. And I kept on talking into my SPIV. That's how the Sinerlesse and I both knew where you'd gone. You told me and I told them. Me and gadgets!'

Mrs Halliday waved across the laboratory. 'Rosie! Good to see you again.'

'You too! Hey, Blondette, didn't I tell you Halo and Al Halo would catch up with you soon?'

Janey grinned. 'No. You told me Mrs Halliday and Alfie would catch up with me. I thought they were baddies!'

'Baddies? Those two? Never! That's why Solomon called them in, I guess, though he didn't have time to tell me.'

'Good people can turn rotten though, Rosie,' said Mrs Halliday. 'It seems Copernicus has double-crossed Solomon.'

G-Mamma almost choked with shock and demanded Mrs Halliday immediately fill her in on Copernicus's treachery.

From the floor where she was trussed up tightly with her sister, Ariel snarled. Alfie looked at her with interest.

'Do you know, I think you could belong in a zoo with a face like that. What do you think, Janey? Mum?'

Mrs Halliday smiled. Now that Janey knew how her teeth had come to be like that, it was no longer threatening but really rather special. 'Well, I think a career behind bars might be all that Miss Rale's fit for now. She certainly won't be coming back to school as a teacher. I think I'd better go and round up the others.'

'Yeah,' said Janey. 'And, Alfie, you get the two ugly sisters into the freezer.'

'No problem, Blonde,' said Alfie, pulling Ariel and Miss Rale along like sacks of potatoes.

'So, Blonde-girl, what was all that I heard about reincarnation?' G-Mamma looked truly impressed. 'Quick thinking, I must say! Zippety split, just like that! I guess you saved your uncle's skin.'

'I suppose so!' said Janey goofily. She suddenly felt shy as she heard her uncle's now familiar, wispy breathing. She couldn't wait to introduce him to G-Mamma, who had served him through all sorts of danger even though she had never met him.

But suddenly Janey felt G-Mamma stiffen and then start to quake. She was staring across the room with a look of terror and disbelief, which transformed into astonishment and deep, deep joy.

'Oh my Lord!' she breathed, shaking like a jelly. 'Oh my sweet serendipitous sunshine! There is reincarnation! There really is!'

'What do you mean, G-Mamma?'

But her godmother wasn't listening. She was too busy bounding across the lab in great wobbling leaps, whispering to herself as though she couldn't believe it, 'Boz! Boz Brown! Oh my cherry-pie eyes, it's Boz Brilliance Brown!'

the other brother

The man Janey had thought was her uncle Solomon gazed across the room at her, his blue eyes filled with a mixture of emotions. Her own feelings churned in the pit of her stomach.

Eventually she forced herself to speak. 'What does she mean? Uncle Sol, what does G-Mamma mean? Are you . . . are you my dad's twin or something? Tell me, please!'

He shook himself free from G-Mamma's embrace and whispered something to her, before crossing over to Janey and taking both her hands in his. 'Oh, Janey, how can I expect you to understand any of this?'

'Well, I'm a SPI, aren't I? Try me!'

He nodded slowly. 'All right. I'll just tell you as straight as I can. I think that's best. Your godmother is right. I'm not Solomon Brown. I'm Boz Brilliance Brown. Your father, Janey.'

Janey's heart hammered. As his words echoed around her head, tears rolled freely down her cheeks. 'What? So why did you pretend to be dead all this time? How could you? Why haven't you been there for me?'

'I've tried, Janey,' said her father gently. 'All through your life I've tried to keep up to date with what's happening to you. I've sent you presents, and I've loved you from afar. I even sent you a message in your puzzle book, telling you that one day this would happen, and we would meet.'

Janey's mind raced back, and she remembered the one puzzle she had never been able to work out. 'Do you mean the dingbat? The one with all the Us?'

'Yes. I know it was very cryptic. It had to be – I couldn't risk other spies finding out I was still alive. It started with a donkey, or an . . .'

'An ass!' shouted Janey. 'It wasn't a horse!'

'Terrible handwriting and very poor drawing skills, I'm afraid,' said her father, looking sheepish. 'But the letter "u" increasing in size meant "as you grow up". And then there was the eye – I, a backwards B, then 2, and finally the word "life".'

Janey thought about it. 'So the whole message was, "As you grow up, I'll be back to life"? No wonder I never got it! I thought the 2 was a Z and the B was an 8. Otherwise I'd have got it straightaway!'

'Well, now I am back to life,' said Boz. 'And you can see what that life is like, Janey. People hunt me down. They chase me. They want to find out what I know, or they want me out of the way. And they do whatever they can, use whoever it takes, to track me down. I can't inflict that life on anyone else, especially my own family. Which is why I've stayed away – until now.'

Janey's head felt leaden. She struggled to take it all in. 'But what about Mum? Didn't you love her?'

'More than I can say. But she was too close to me. She knew too much; it put her in terrible danger. As soon as I knew we were expecting a baby – you, Janey – I had to do something to protect you both. And when Reg and I were in the accident, but I survived, I took my chance to disappear. I needed to let you and Gina start a new life, a different one.'

'Did . . . did you really kill Ariel's father?'

'Of course not!' said Boz. 'When we discovered the wood frog's secret together, Reg was the first to offer himself up for the experiment. Anyway, we didn't get the calculations quite right. He froze too quickly, and you know what happens then, Janey. He asked me, if anything happened, to scatter his crystals at the North Pole – I think he wanted to feel like Santa Claus. The Sol's Lols picture is very like him. I miss him still.'

Janey watched, mesmerized, as her father talked. 'So, who . . . where is Uncle Solomon?'

With a little laugh, her father ran his fingers through his hair. 'Ah. Sol. Well, this is where it gets complicated. You see, I come from a long line of spies. So, from the moment I was born, my family pretended I had a brother. It's quite common in spy dynasties. No one ever met him or saw him, but we fed people stories of his illness, being sent away to school, then into the military and eventually abroad for his work. Well, people believed us. There never was a Solomon Brown. Then, when I needed a new identity after I faked my death, there it was. Ready for me to step into.'

Janey sighed. It was all so weird. Too much. But she supposed that one day she'd get used to it all. 'Right now,' she said, 'I'm just glad that you're here, and you can come back home with me, and Mum will remember everything, and we can be a family again. The Browns. We can even invent a sister for me, so I can carry on being a SPI.'

But even as she spoke, Janey sensed her father's alarm. He was shaking his head, his brow furrowed with concern. 'No, Janey. It's just not possible. I thought I'd explained. Your mother must never know. She must never remember. It's too dangerous, for me, certainly, but especially for you.'

'But . . . we've dealt with the Sinerlesse Group. And we've kept your secret hidden. All we need to do now is destroy the files, isn't it? I can't find you after all this time just to have you disappear again!' Janey was shivering, so furious and upset that she wanted to fling herself at her father and beat his chest with her fists.

'Better hurry, Boz-babe,' said G-Mamma. 'We have company.'

When Janey's father heard the voice that was approaching, his calm expression faltered. 'Gina!'

He was right. Janey could hear her mother shouting to someone else, 'I don't *know* why she'd be at the Wildlife Park in the middle of the night. But I suspect that ridiculous woman is something to do with it. So that's why we've followed her here. What *is* that peculiar-looking cat doing? It must have escaped from a cage. Hurry up, James!'

'But what are you doing, Jean?' Uncle James was asking.

'Well, I couldn't tell you why, but I'm pretty sure this is the way we get in. I must find Janey!'

Frantically, Boz Brilliance Brown looked from Janey to G-Mamma and back again. The voices were hovering overhead, and meanwhile the Halos were herding the remaining Sinerlesse members into the freezer. 'I have to go!' he said urgently.

'No! D-Dad! Don't!'

He swept her up into his arms and squeezed for what felt like the longest moment of Janey's life. 'I can't stay, Janey . . .'

Janey shook her head miserably. Over their heads, the frog tube was starting to rattle. And as her mother's feet appeared at ceiling level, Janey could hardly believe what she was saying. But somehow it felt right. 'I know! Go! Just go!'

'Don't forget what I told you before, Janey,' he said, hugging her fiercely. 'No time to explain now. But the Ruler will tell you. Then make sure all traces are destroyed.' Janey nodded. 'And Al,' Boz Brown continued, turning to Alfie, 'freeze them slowly, Spylet. I want them whole.'

'Yes, sir,' was Alfie's reply. He and his mother turned their backs discreetly and fiddled with the controls next to the freezer as Boz seized a pair of cylinders and strapped them on to his back.

'Dad, one thing,' pleaded Janey.

'Yes?' He turned to look at her, burning to get away, but longing to stay.

'Don't make me forget everything, like you did with Mum. I want to remember.'

Their eyes locked, and a lifetime of unspoken words passed between them. Finally he smiled and nodded. 'I need you to remember, Janey. You're my SPI now. Take care, always.'

He yanked the cord across his chest and, in a plume of purple smoke, burst out through an opening in the roof of the building and up into the night sky.

Janey watched his feet disappear just as her mother's touched on to the floor of the SPI-lab. Uncle James was right behind, trying desperately to shake off Trouble, who clung to his leg, shedding yellow and brown hairs all over his tuxedo.

'I don't know where this animal appeared from. It's been practically attached to me since I left the ball!'

'You!' yelled Janey's mum at G-Mamma. 'What on earth has been going on? Is that Janey behind you?'

Before Janey had time to answer, G-Mamma swivelled two of her enormous rings around on her fingers so that they sat inside each palm. Reaching out her hands, she pressed a ring into one arm of both Janey's mother and Uncle James. They instantly looked dazed and confused. Mrs Brown peered woozily at her daughter.

'Janey? My Janey Brown. Is that you?' Her voice

sounded thick, as though her tongue had suddenly doubled in size.

And Janey, smoothing out her ponytail as she stood tall in her SPI-suit, smiled gently. 'No. No, I'm sorry. You must have mistaken me for someone else. My name is Blonde: Jane Blonde. I expect your Janey is tucked up at home in bed.'

'Oh,' said her mother vaguely, before she slumped into a mound on the floor on top of Uncle James.

Brushing away a tear, Janey turned to G-Mamma, who was flattening Trouble's quiff. The cat broke away from her and ran, mewing happily, straight to Janey's side.

Janey looked at him with a sad smile. 'Trouble,' she said, 'let's go home.'

the ruler

G-Mamma drove everybody home in the Wildlife Park minibus.

'Great,' said Alfie as he climbed in the back. 'We'll be really inconspicuous going up the motorway in a van with big grey ears and a trunk.'

'It's that or a real elephant,' said his mother, settling in beside him. 'Be quiet and go to sleep.'

'So who is this ruler you have to destroy?' G-Mamma asked Janey under her breath. 'Because I gotta tell you, Blonde-girl, sensational though you are, I wouldn't fancy your chances of removing all trace of old Copper Knickers! Double-crossing doughnut.'

Janey looked round to check the other passengers were all sound asleep. 'I don't think it's a "who",' she said, 'but I need to check something when we get home.'

After dropping off the Halos, G-Mamma and Janey managed to drag the brain-wiped bodies of Janey's mum and Uncle James into Janey's house and settle them down for the night. In her own room, Janey rummaged in her school bag, then zipped once more through the fireplace into the SPI-lab.

'This is one of the presents from Uncle . . . from my father,' she said, placing her pencil case on the bench top. 'And I think this ruler must be . . . well, *the* Ruler.'

They both stared at it. It was an unremarkable metal ruler, pretty short, and in inches instead of centimetres.

'How do we destroy that?' asked G-Mamma.

Janey grinned. 'Just like the rest of Project Crystal Clear. We melt it.'

'OK.' G-Mamma lit a Bunsen burner and pushed it towards Janey. 'Off you go, Blondette.'

Janey took a deep breath. This was something precious her father had sent her, and she was going to obliterate it. 'Bye, SPI-buy,' she whispered, and gave it a kiss.

'Oooo, good rap!' said G-Mamma. 'Bye, SPI-buy . . . bye SPI-b—'

She stopped short. With a quiet hum, four beams of light had shot out of the ruler and projected themselves on to the ceiling. An image was shimmering into being.

Janey gulped.

'Good noddy noodles!' shouted G-Mamma. 'It's a LipSPICK. I've never even seen one! A Lip-activated SPI-Camera Kilobank. You can download on to these at any distance. Fantastic work, Blonde!'

Janey pointed sadly at the picture. 'Look. It's my dad.'

There was Boz Brilliance Brown, sitting in his swivel

chair in the Sol's Lols office. He was patting a small tabby cat. 'That's Trouble!' shouted G-Mamma.

With a pounding heart, Janey listened to what her father was saying.

'It's gone too far. I can hardly believe what I've discovered. The only remaining formulae for Project Crystal Clear are on this file. It must be destroyed. Here's what I've created, Spylet.' He reached down towards Trouble, his face so close to the camera that Janey could clearly see the bright blue of his eyes. Then he leaned past the cat and pointed to something on the floor, something that Trouble clearly didn't like. It was a large brown field mouse.

'Solomon told me Trouble hated mice,' said G-Mamma.

'I'm not surprised,' said Janey. 'Look at it.' Instead of scurrying off, the mouse huddled back on its haunches before leaping out of Trouble's way in a great arc. The camera followed it as it sprang around the desk.

Boz looked sombre on the screen. 'This mouse . . . used to be a frog. A North American wood frog. I've turned it into another species through an intensified Crystal Clarification Process. I've made new life. If someone finds out how to do this with humans, the planet is doomed. All the formulae are on this file and exist nowhere else in physical form. Destroy this file. This secret cannot get out.' With that, the image flickered and disappeared.

Janey and G-Mamma were silent for a long

time, staring at the Ruler, letting the enormity of Boz's discovery sink in. Janey's made-up reincarnation ruse wasn't that far from the truth. Janey could see that if this discovery got into the wrong hands, the outcome could be terrifying. Finally she picked up the Ruler. 'Great, so I've got to destroy my only picture of my dad.'

G-Mamma nodded. 'I know, Blonde. But you're a wonderful Spylet. Do what you have to do.'

So Janey put on her Girl-gauntlet and held the Ruler in the orange-blue flame of the Bunsen burner. As the metal hit the heat it evaporated, disappearing into nothing. All that remained was the tiny dot Janey had held between her thumb and forefinger.

'It's done,' she said. 'It's over. Solomon's secret is safe forever.'

G-Mamma nodded. 'And you'd better go, Blonde. Your mum will be waking up soon. Catch you later.'

Janey slipped back through to her own bedroom. The tiny disc of metal was still attached to her finger. Gently she kissed it and, as she had secretly hoped, a picture flashed on to the ceiling, just for a second or two – her father, his blue eyes crinkled, leaning over Trouble, saying, ' . . . what I've created.'

Janey watched it over and over until she fell asleep.

brilliance

'Why isn't Miss Rale coming with us?' shouted Andrew Marsden. He was being extra boisterous to prove what fun he could still be even though his usual place next to Alfie had been taken.

Mrs Halliday stood up at the front of the coach and clapped her hands. All the children turned to face her, apart from Alfie and Janey. Janey was too busy wondering what everyone must be thinking; she had suddenly gone from having no friends at all to being offered the seat next to the Class Superstar, by the Class Superstar himself.

'Well, as Andrew has asked the question, I suppose I should let you all know,' said Mrs Halliday loudly. 'Miss Rale has had to leave the school rather abruptly. We'll be finding a new teacher for you, but in the meantime I will be keeping an eye on you myself. And while I'm on my feet, I think we should take the opportunity to thank Janey Brown for organizing this trip to the Wildlife Park. Her uncle, Solomon Brown, is the proprietor, and he has very kindly allowed us free access for the day. Furthermore, it seems we are to be the first to visit the newly refurbished Amphibian House. Three cheers for our Janey. Hip hip!' Three cheers straggled down the coach.

It was only a week since Janey had last been in the Amphibian House and discovered the truth about so many things. The next morning she'd been woken by her mum.

'I must go to the doctor's,' she'd groaned to Janey. 'I've had another one of those weird dreams! And I can't explain what Uncle James is doing sleeping on the sofa downstairs.'

'Oh, I wanted to come home after that ball Uncle James took me to, remember?' lied Janey. 'We got his car to drop us off, and then . . . and then his chauffeur and cleaner resigned.'

'Really?' Her mother leaned against the edge of the sink, looking green. 'Well, I don't remember any of that. Think I'm going mad. I'm going to have to call Miss Lear and cry off work this morning.'

Rolling her eyes as she followed Mrs Brown down the stairs, Janey launched into another lie. 'Well, I think you were sleepy when we got home, so you won't recall that she'd left a message saying the . . . the cleaning business had folded so she won't be needing you any more. And . . . um . . . and she's leaving the country with Freda, I mean Freddie, so you won't see her again.'

'But she hasn't paid me!'

'I think that's the least of your problems,' muttered Janey under her breath.

Uncle James had stirred and was looking at himself in

disgust in the mirror over the mantelpiece. 'Typical of small businesses. Although how she could afford to throw a party like that if the company was going under, I don't know. You should have seen the place, Jean. Thought for a while I might have found the new Mrs Bell.'

Janey thought quickly. 'Hey, Uncle James, don't you think Mum would be good at running a business like that? She could hire out people to be, you know, housekeepers and chauffeurs and minders.'

Uncle James nodded appreciatively. 'Do you know, Janey, you're right! Must be a gap in the market now that St Earl's has gone under. I could set you up and you could run it, Jean. Well done, Janey. Good focus!'

'Well, you sort my life out among yourselves,' mumbled Mrs Brown. 'Must admit it's a good idea though, Janey. But right now, I'm going to be sick.'

And now Janey was on the way back to her uncle's wildlife park. As they passed the plywood animals along the road leading up to the large iron gates she exchanged a secret smile with Alfie. He'd been a good friend to her since that night. Best of all, he had introduced her into his group of friends, telling everyone that mad Freddie Lear, Bin Boy, had been leaving those notes because he was jealous of her. Janey hoped that one day they'd be close enough for her to ask Alfie about his father, but knew that day hadn't arrived yet.

Now the class was trooping through the park, oohing and aahing at the endangered animals prowling the compounds around them. Midway through the morning, Mrs Halliday turned to the group.

'Now, class, we've reached the new Amphibian House for the official opening. Unfortunately Solomon Brown can't be here today, but he's sent one of his key employees, Rosie Biggenham, to cut the ribbon with Janey.'

The class clapped obediently as Janey joined G-Mamma at the festooned doorway.

G-Mamma coughed delicately. 'Hope you don't mind, but I've written a little poem, well, more of a song, well, kind of a rap, to mark this Brownalicious event.'

'Oh no,' whispered Janey, but G-Mamma had already started to clap and shake her hips.

'We love the Brown family, you know it's true!
Though I think that Mother's got a bit to do.
But this girly-girl is coming through,
And yo! She'll surprise all o' you!
Goooooooooo, Janey!'

Alfie raised his eyebrows at Janey as she glowed bright red. The class whooped and clapped, practising the rap among themselves.

'Go to it, Blonde-girl!' hissed G-Mamma delightedly, preening more than a little. Janey couldn't stop a huge grin spreading across her face.

Between them, G-Mamma and Janey levered the huge scissors into position and sliced the ribbon in two.

Janey was first through the door, with Alfie, Andrew and the others in quick pursuit. She made her way to the North American wood frog cabinet, buried in the depths of the Amphibian House. As she reached the spot she turned to Alfie, stunned.

It was gone.

In its place was an enormous and impressive display. Sealed behind layers of heavy mesh, a family of snarling creatures glared back at her. They were, according to the plaque, a group of mink. The smallest mink looked particularly vicious, displaying two rows of neat, gnashing teeth that looked as though they could tear a limb off a tiger without a second thought. As it clapped eyes on Janey, it threw itself against the metal, thrashing demonically.

'Calm down, little mink!' said Janey. 'No point getting all upset.' She leaned in closer. 'It's your own fault, after all,' she whispered.

The mink went wild.

'Hey, these are mammals, aren't they?' asked Andrew. 'What are they doing in here?'

Mrs Halliday was looking at a plaque further around the display cabinet. 'Well, I suppose Mr Brown can do what he likes in his own wildlife park. I think it's a quite incredible display, wherever it is, don't you, Andrew? Particularly when it was inspired by one of your own classmates. Come and look at this, Janey.'

Confused, Janey tore her eyes away from the smallest mink and moved around the cabinet to

Mrs Halliday's side. She saw her headmistress brush away a tear as she gestured towards a small silver plate screwed into the wood at the base of the cabinet.

It had only three words on it. 'For Janey – "Brilliance".'

The other children had surged forward to look too. 'Brilliance? Is that the name of the display? Pretty cool having your own piece of a wildlife park! Did your uncle do that just for you?'

As they spoke, Janey's head suddenly cleared with that peculiar brightness of her Spylet moments. Slowly she nodded.

'I think so. To make sure I always remember.'

Alfie looked puzzled. 'You didn't get brain-wiped, did you?' he whispered to her, pulling her to one side. 'What else would you need to remember?'

'Just who I am, Al.' Linking her arm through his, Janey smiled as she walked away. 'Just need to remember who I am.'

G-Mamma, with a hand on each Spylet's shoulder, winked broadly. 'You're lovely normal Janey Brown, hey, honey-child?'

Janey threw back her pale brown hair and laughed. 'That's right, G-Mamma. Janey Brown. I'm just Janey Brown.'

And for the time being, she was.

A selected list of titles available from Macmillan Children's Books

The prices shown below are correct at the time of going to press. However, Macmillan Publishers reserves the right to show new retail prices on covers, which may differ from those previously advertised.

Georgia Byng

Molly Moon's Incredible Book of Hypnotism	0 330 39985 3	£4.99
Molly Moon Stops the World	0 330 41577 8	£4.99
Molly Moon's Hypnotic Time-travel Adventure	0 330 45461 6	£5.99

Ellen Potter

Olivia Kidney	0 330 42079 8	£4.99
Olivia Kidney Stops for No One	0 330 42080 1	£4.99
Olivia Kidney Hot on the Trail	0 330 44158 8	£9.99

All Pan Macmillan titles can be ordered from our website, www.panmacmillan.com, or from your local bookshop and are also available by post from:

Bookpost, PO Box 29, Douglas, Isle of Man IM99 1BQ
Credit cards accepted. For details:
Telephone: 01624 677237
Fax: 01624 670923
Email: bookshop@enterprise.net
www.bookpost.co.uk

Free postage and packing in the United Kingdom